THE ASCENDANT PATH

SCHOLAR

Contents

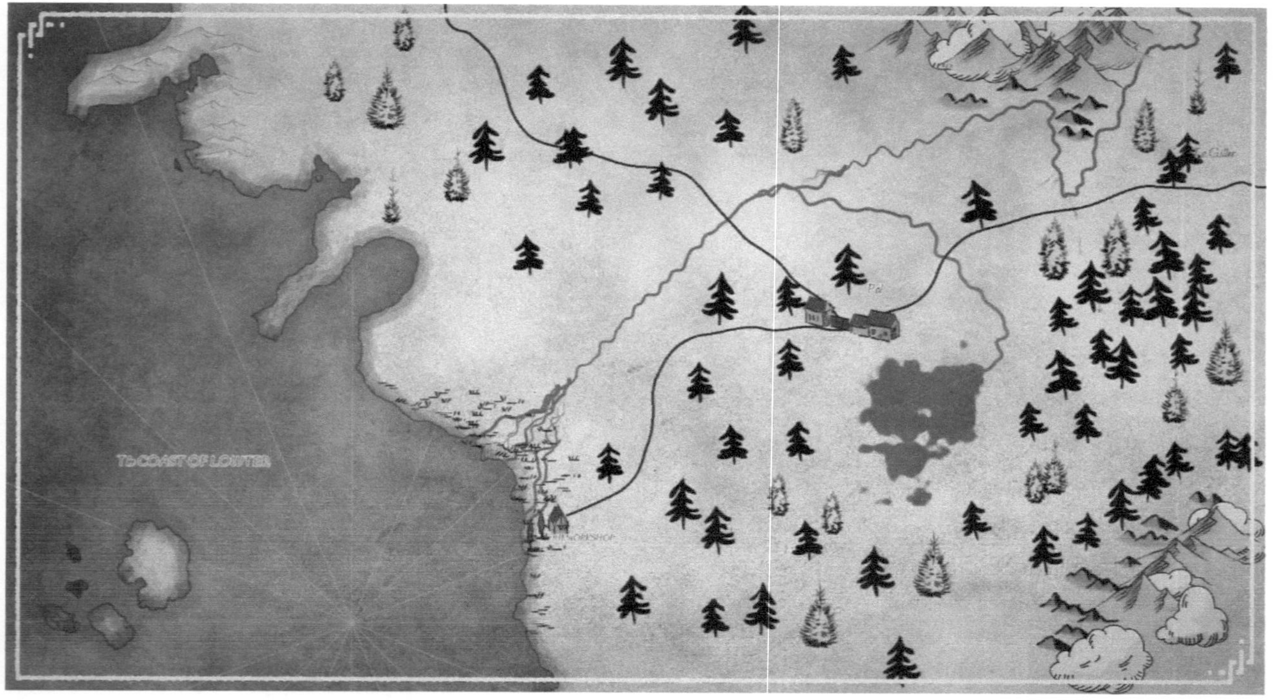

The Coast of Lohmer
HORSESHOE

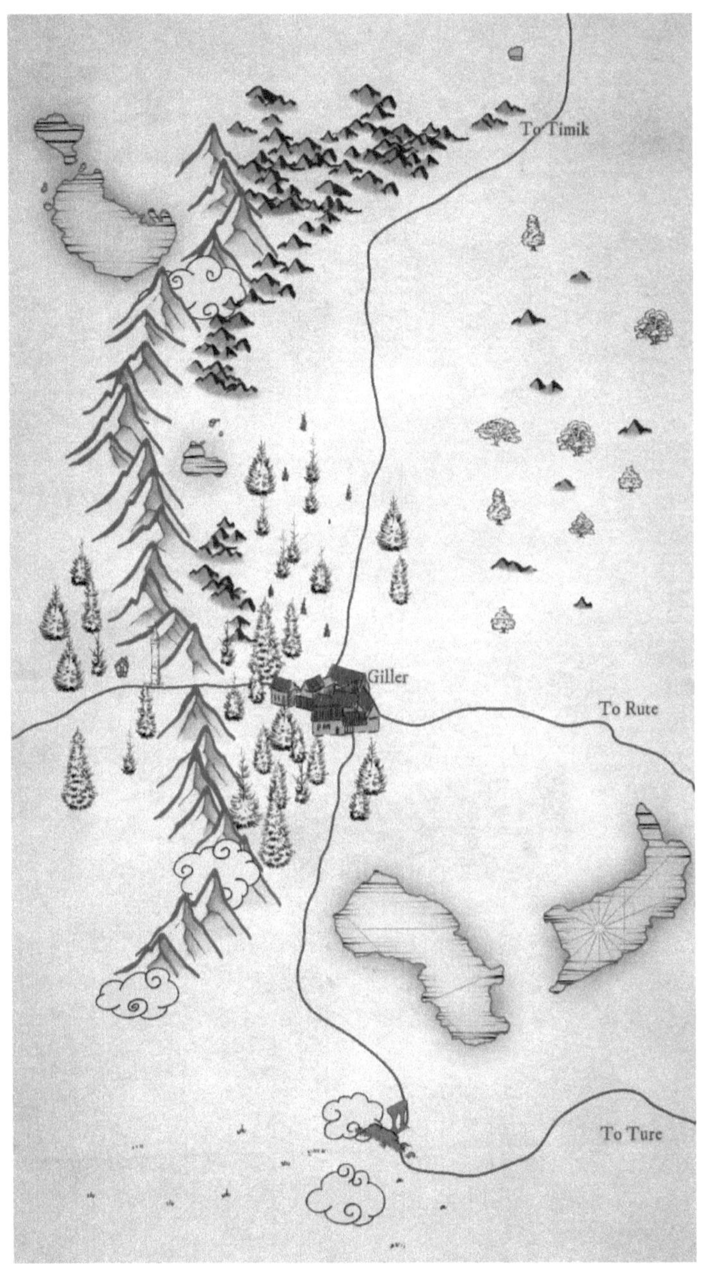

To Timik
To Rute
To Ture
Giller

Chapter One

Layten watched the road leading to the house, his house, with a focus and glare that made his jaw ache. Where were they? What was taking so long? Wiping his hands for the twentieth time this morning, he glared at the road again, as if to force the appearance of his traveling companions. Which was, of course, impossible. One of the riders was an Anchor. Magic wouldn't work on an Anchor. Not that he'd ever touch magic. It was evil. Wrong.

"Layten, if you clench your jaw any tighter you will break it." His mother, Reina, shook her head, but her voice was cheerful enough, now at least. It hadn't been last night. He'd heard her crying softly outside. It had been that way ever since he'd decided to leave. He'd dreamed of being a scholar. Of learning things. Books and ink. Marking rods, and hidden history and knowledge. It had been all he'd ever wanted.

His father hadn't been much better. He'd always wanted Layten to stay here. To be a papermaker. Not just ANY papermaker, but a Grayread. The finest paper and scroll maker in all northern Alos. It was the only reason the Anchor was even coming here. It was time to replace the warding circle. That Layten would NOT look at. He'd hated the thing all his life. The jet-black circle clung to the pole it was strung up on, its black surface shifting and swirling if you stared at it enough. That was odd, and unsettling for sure. But it wasn't the worst part.

The fact that the closer you got to the circle, the cooler it got wasn't the worst thing either. He'd almost been tempted to stand under it some days, here on the edge of the great saltmarsh in the heights of summer. That was odd, but it wasn't what made him hate the thing. What made him hate the thing was the sound. It wasn't supposed to make a sound. No one else ever mentioned it. But to Layten, it made a sound. The sound of a person screaming in agony and fear. Repeatedly. It was faint, so faint that he sometimes couldn't make it out. But it always returned. He hated it. Over the years the only way he'd found to get around it was to keep his distance, and never mention the sound. The last time he had, his mother had turned as grey as the marsh mud they used to grow the reed beds.

But the warding circle did its job. Keeping the grounds of his parents' workshop, his house, and the reed beds all safe. Safe from magic. Safe from the creatures that spawn from that dark force. But every few years, it had to be replaced. An Anchor would come.

Layten clearly remembered the last time an Anchor had come. A slight figure had ridden up, flanked by two hard-eyed guards clad in the livery of the Church of Sartum. Blood red and silver, and not a speck of dirt or mud on either of them. But it had been the Anchor that had drawn his attention more. Robed and with a large hood covering its face, he'd not even been sure if it was a man or a woman. Not that it mattered.

An Anchor was an Anchor. They carried the staff. Black and oily, like the warding circle only longer and straight. Anchors sought out magic and destroyed it. Layten wasn't sure how. No one ever spoke of it. He'd asked of course. All children did. Sometimes the parent would shush them. Other times they'd say something fantastical and silly. But others, others would hunker down and speak in whispered tones. About how Anchors always slowly go crazy.

How the magic they take in eats at them, driving them mad. How finally at the end, they were taken to the High Temple of Sartum in far off Ture and vanished forever. Layten had watched the Anchor with a hefty dose of fear and loathing. Magic was EVIL. To be willing to even interact with it was suspicious. But the Anchors kept them safe.

The last time the Anchor had come, Layten had been sent away as soon as the Anchor had dismounted. His father had gruffly told him to go inside and stay there until he'd been called back out. And to not look out any window or door.

The Anchor had laughed at that... a low wheezing thing, but right at the end, a giggle had escaped, a giggle that sent a shiver up Layten's back at the sound. And now, here he was waiting for them to arrive again, desperate for them to arrive again. And as far as he was concerned, it was a waste of time.

"I still don't understand why I must go with them. I can go to town by myself. And from there talk to a trader or two and get to the House of Knowledge in Timik."

Layten knew what the answer would be. It had been the same answer he'd gotten every time he'd complained.

"It's not safe," his father Unil grumbled. "Too many sightings lately. With the warding needing to be refreshed. Old Tark saw something in the swamp the other day. I don't need you being dragged off."

"Tark sees things because he chews sweetgrass," Layten snorted.

"You live as long as Tark and had the life he's had, you'd chew sweetgrass as well." His father shook his finger at Layten. "Tark's been here since I started this place. He's been here your whole life, Layten. Show some respect."

Layten nodded but didn't look his father in the eye. Tark wasn't bad, but the man did spend any time he could slightly out of his mind from sweetgrass. Tark had sworn once when Layten was a child that he'd seen a figure right at the edge of the ward, just past the last reed bed that looked exactly like Layten, if Layten had green skin, bright blue eyes, and was dripping water and mud. Layten had refused to go anywhere near the reed beds for over a month after that.

"You can still stay here you know. You don't have to go. I'm getting older, and no one else knows the work like you. You are my blood." Unil's voice interrupted Layten's thoughts.

"You know it's all I've ever wanted. I'm not cut out for this place. I want to know things, understand things. I don't want to spend my life at the edge of a swamp and avoiding the glares of people in town." Layten shrugged in response.

"I know. I know. I had to ask one more time." Unil thumped the wall twice. "Don't worry Layten, they will be here soon."

Layten wasn't really worried. Just impatient. "Thanks. And thanks again... for helping me get into the House of Knowledge."

"Well, if you aren't going to be a papermaker, at least you can use the stuff." His father waved a hand away. Layten knew there was more to it, but that was enough. His father had used his connections to get him into the Scholars. Not that Layten had only gotten in based on that. But it had helped. If the son of the best paper and scroll maker in the North wants to be a scholar, you tend to let them, since everything you do is based on paper.

Layten knew all that and was grateful. But right now, he wanted to be gone. He wanted to be down that road, not stuck here waiting for an Anchor. He wasn't afraid of anything the road would hold for him; he was sure it would be safe. This was Lowter. It was in the North. Safe and away from the wrongness and debauchery that the south reveled in.

"There." His mother's voice spoke. "See them there?" Her arm stretched out pointing down the road. And she was right. Finally, the Anchor had arrived. Three figures and four horses were heading down the road to the house and workshop.

Was that final horse for him? He had a horse already. It wasn't as nice as the horses the Anchor and his guards had, but Gumshoe was a steady horse, and one that Layten was comfortable riding. Quickly though he realized the truth when he spied the large, wrapped bundle strapped to its side. That last horse was carrying the new warding circle. As the riders approached, Layten's father went out onto the porch with his mother to await them.

"Layten, come out here." Unil waved him out. "You're too old to be hiding out in the house."

Layten felt his face get warm. There was a moment of fear that he pushed away and stepped out with his parents. His father was right, he just… "I'm not afraid," he said softly.

"Good. Now be respectful. Anchors are unpredictable sometimes, you know that." Unil reached out and squeezed Layten's shoulder. "You will be fine though." The Anchor that approached them was not the one that had come last time, Layten was sure of that. That one had been slight of build. This one was broad-shouldered to the point of almost being silly looking. He was wearing a hood and cloak that completely covered his face, which was odd. The Anchor sort of slid off the horse, a fluid motion that spoke to years of practice at least.

Layten heard a sudden intake of breath from both his parents. His mother's face had gone sweaty even in this cool morning air, and his fathers was even more shocked than hers. Why were they so surprised? The Anchor approached them, the customary hood hiding his face.

"Unil. Reina." The Anchor's voice was raspy, but somehow oddly familiar. Layten couldn't quite place it, but it felt somehow like a voice he should know.

"You." Unil finally spoke. "Why are you here?"

"Layten. That's why I'm here." The voice came again, with a hitch that made Layten's skin crawl. Like a trace of a giggle or laugh was about to come out.

"What do you mean?" His mother Reina dropped her eyes. "Sorry, Anchor."

"No offense taken." The Anchor paused. "I came to make sure he made it to the House of Knowledge safely. And to replace the warding circle of course."

"Father? What is going on? Mother?" Layten was more than confused. This Anchor knew him? He spoke like… he was familiar with him. How could an Anchor know who he was? The idea grew into an icy knot in his chest. The mere thought that an Anchor would know him…no. Layten pushed that idea aside. He would not be afraid.

"Layten Grayread. You will go with me and the guards when we leave. You will stay with us until we arrive at the House of Knowledge, where you will join the scholars. On the road you will listen to any orders given when it comes to safety. Do you understand?" The Anchor had turned to him, the hood hiding his face, but that voice… it was so… familiar.

"Do you understand?" the Anchor asked again, a hint of some feeling in it that made Layten's hands grow damp and cold again.

"Yes, Anchor." Layten lowered his eyes, not even wanting to give the appearance of not listening.

"Good." The Anchor turned to the two guards and pointed at the old warding circle. "That goes. Put up the new one and I'll do the ritual."

The two guards moved without a word, one giving Layten a nod as she walked past, her eyes holding something akin to pity in them as she looked at him. Layten just felt himself growing more and more confused. What was going on? Who was this Anchor?

Chapter Two

"Mother? Who is this Anchor?" Layten whispered to her ear as soon as he could. Something had obviously shocked her; she was a short but sturdy woman. Skin browned from years of work outside. But now her skin was almost pale, and a slight tremble seemed to come to her as she watched the Anchor stand off to one side, talking to his father.
"Don't ask such questions. Don't… ask." Reina looked away; her hand half raised to cover her mouth. "Just do whatever you are told, Layten. Do NOT argue for once?"
Layten had never seen her this way. Oh, she'd gotten onto him many times for arguing, but the tone of fear was unknown to him. At least from her. His mother's eyes locked onto his, wide. "I won't. I promise."
Layten's words seemed to help some as she gave a nod. "Good. Now, go inside and get drinks for the guards. Offer food. Go!" His mother shooed him inside but kept her eyes on his father and the Anchor.
Layten did as she asked. It was obvious she wanted to keep him as far from the Anchor as possible. At least right now. But he was to be leaving with this person they obviously knew? How did his parents know an Anchor? People in town would be scandalized if they knew. Maybe that was it. They were tolerated but not loved. Even though they had their own warding circle, Layten knew there had always been whispers about them.

Living this close to the marshes, and what could be seen outside the protection of the circle was enough to make almost anyone have second thoughts about someone. Layten never spoke about it, but he'd caught glimpses over the years of things out there. He always told himself it was just the mists that rose off the low water every morning, but mist doesn't wave and make faces.

Layten pushed that memory away. He was going to the House of Knowledge. He would be a scholar. He just had to put up with this strange twist in his journey. That was all. He filled two mugs with cold little beer, and walked back outside, keeping his eyes forward, though he could still see right at the edge of his vision both his parents talking and pointing at the house, at him, and at the Anchor. His mother was certainly on edge, and his father... his father had the look of a man who'd been running from a fate and just found out he hadn't run fast enough.

"Here. Cold drinks." Layten approached the two guards, handing them each a mug. "Long ride. I assume you didn't stop at the village?"

The female guard smiled and took her mug with an arched eyebrow. "Was that a village? Back in Vili that would have been a single house."

"You're from Vili??" Layten had never met anyone from Vili. He'd met a few traders over the years from different places, even a few from the border countries of Hanam and Gilik. But most were from here, Lowter. Boring, dull, Lowter.

"Yes." The guard took a long drink. "Needed a change of pace. Never thought I'd end up in Lowter, in the great marsh, guarding an Anchor."

"Hush, Binin," the male guard muttered and took his drink. "I am Protector Wilk. That talkative person is Protector Binin. That is all you need to know."

"Don't mind Wilk. He's permanently annoyed." Protector Binin shook her head. "So, you will be coming with us from what I understand?"

Layten nodded. He wondered where Wilk was from, but decided not to ask, at least right now. He didn't seem the sort to share information, at least not with someone he'd just met. "Yes. I'm going to the House of Knowledge to be a scholar."

Wilk made a snorting noise but said nothing and moved off a bit, drinking his little beer. "Protector? Is that because you're with the Anchor?"

"Yes. Guards assigned to Anchors have that title, and… duties." Binin's smile dropped. "This Anchor is nice enough, as Anchors go. But…" Protector Binin's face hardened for a second. "Just remember, Anchors have a job. A horrible job."

"Layten!" His father Unil's voice rang out. "Stop bothering the guards. Come here."

Layten turned back to where his parents and the Anchor had been. His mother was nowhere in sight now, she must have returned to the house. His father's mouth was set in a very thin line, he was gritting his teeth hard, based on the knots of muscle on his face.

"Coming." Layten walked over, keeping his eyes off the Anchor.

The Anchor himself was still cloaked and silent but was facing Layten. He was still strange. Layten had never been this close to an Anchor before and had no idea what he was supposed to feel. But it made his skin crawl. The staff he carried was worse. Looking at it he felt the same sense of abject horror and terror that he did when too near the warding circle, but this was worse. Sharper somehow.

"Layten. This Anchor... is ..." his father's voice broke, as if he had a hard time saying the name.

"Fean." The Anchor spoke again, finally, his voice hinting at something. "You will call me Anchor Fean."

"Fean?" Layten knew that was a Palnorian name. Palnor. Both blessed and cursed, Ture and the western parts of that land were the home of the Church of Sartum, and oddly, the Anchorhold. And the eastern parts were held to be cursed and of ill repute. That was where the Betrayer was from.

"Yes. Fean." The Anchor coughed a few times. "But you will call me ANCHOR Fean. Do not forget that."

"Yes, Anchor Fean." Layten lowered his eyes. He doubted strongly he would speak to this Anchor even once if he could help it.

"Stay, Layten. And watch. This is important." Until leaned in. "It is time you know how the circles work." Anchor Fean turned to the two Protectors. "Put down the drinks. It is time."

To their credit the two Protectors did so, at once. They lowered the existing circle quickly, placed it on the ground, and unpacked the new circle from a bundle on the Anchor's horse. This they took and placed on top of the old circle, somehow perfectly balancing the two round-edged things without effort.

Anchor Fean walked to the circles and stepped inside them, the circles barely big enough for both his feet to enter. He pulled a small dagger out from under his robe. Greyish black, the edge seemed to trail a faint red mist, like the old legends of the Bloodmist from before the unsundering.

"It is time, Reina," his father called out.

His mother stepped out of the house, and she had changed. Her normal long-sleeved shirt was gone, and her arms were bare. His father rolled up his sleeves as well. "Stay here, Layten. Do nothing but watch," his father whispered one more time.

Layten felt a chill move up his back, and for a moment felt sick to his stomach. He felt disgusted by whatever was happening here. This was wrong. This was evil. It had to be. This was magic! But it couldn't be magic. It COULDN'T be. He wanted to turn his back on the whole thing, turn his back and pretend he wasn't seeing this. Whatever it was.

Both his parents stopped just outside the rings, and both offered the Anchor an arm. Fean pressed the dagger to his lips, cutting them both. A trickle of dark red blood moved down his chin, but less than there should have been. Much less. And the look on the Anchor's face was worse. His eyes rolled back in his head and a giggle escaped him again, a ragged sound, harsh in the way a laugh should never be, at least to Layten.

The Anchor's mouth snapped shut, and with a single motion he cut both offered arms, and blood fountained forth. Layten sprung forward; he wasn't going to let this monster, this THING, kill his parents! He hadn't even seen the Protectors move close to him, but he only had managed a single step when two sets of hands grabbed him and held him firmly. "HOLD," Protector Wilk's voice hissed. Layten tried for a moment to twist out of their grasp. He wasn't weak, but he wasn't a match for two Protectors.

He only tried for a moment though, as his eyes beheld a horrible sight. A white fog seemed to flow from both his parents, swirling around the three figures and the two warding circles. No, not white, greyer. Grey with leering faces, and strange forms. Forms that writhed in pain or ecstasy, Layten wasn't sure. Then a scream, a horrible scream came forth. His mother screamed. His father screamed. And another voice. Not the Anchor, not the Protectors, not himself. But from the warding circle. A scream of unending agony. A scream that went on, with no pause to breathe. A scream that echoed in Layten's head.

The sound grew, drowning out his parents. A memory came to him, a memory of this sound. And somehow, forgetting it. How had he ever forgotten this?? He'd heard this sound the last time the circle had been replaced, and the time before that, and before that. How had he ever forgotten? The scream stopped, suddenly. The grey mist, now streaked with the red of fresh blood seemed to enter the new warding circle, sucked into it like smoke escaping.

His parents stood there, silent, the wounds on their arms gone, as if they had never been there. If Layten hadn't seen the cut, he would have never thought it had happened. What was all this? The horrid metallic taste of bile covered his tongue, threatening to make him sick once more.

Chapter Three

Layten watched in silent horror as both of his parents walked away from the warding circles and this Anchor Fean. From here he could see both were unsteady, and at least twice his mother had to grab his father's arm to steady herself. Yet, both kept moving, walking towards the main workshop, and both pointedly did not look at Layten.

The Anchor simply stood there for a moment, his robe trembling. There was no wind, there usually wasn't this time of day. The breezes that came in from the marsh came in the late afternoon, and it wasn't even lunchtime yet. Lunchtime. The mere idea of eating made Layten want to be sick. He had more questions than he could concentrate on, but he knew he wasn't going to get any answers right now.

Finally, the Anchor stepped out of the warding circles, and quickly made his way to his horse, and removed a small pouch from a saddle bag. He vanished with the pouch behind a building, saying nothing to anyone. As for the two Protectors, they finally let Layten go, went to their own horses, each retrieving a set of leather gloves, and hung the new warding circle in its place.

Layten could feel the change in the air as it rose, blocking any magic from being nearby. A calm settled over him, yet he still didn't like the circle, and if his eyes met it, he could feel an echo of pain and terror still. Stronger even since the circle was new.

The old circle was left on the ground, discarded. That was strange but seemed minor compared to everything else. He needed answers. His parents were the obvious choice to start with. He half ran over to them both, watching as they both turned to him, finally. His father squared his shoulders as if he half expected Layten to attack them. His mother Reina wiped her hands on her work apron four or five times, her face pale.

"What. Was. That?" Layten asked as he stopped in front of them. "Why did I hear screaming? What happened? Why do I remember this happening before suddenly? What is going on???"

Unil and Reina looked at each other before answering. "We hid those memories from you," his mother finally said. "It was better."

"Hid memories?? How?" Layten felt sick. That had to mean magic. And magic was wrong! EVIL! How could this be happening? An Anchor doing magic? His parents being involved with this?

"With help." The Anchor's voice came from behind Layten, who turned to see the robed and hooded figure standing there. The only thing that looked different was his right hand, which was bandaged now, and a slight tinge of fresh blood could be seen staining the bandage. Had he hurt himself in whatever blasphemous ritual that had been?

"Magic is evil!" Layten nearly spat the words.

"That's not what the teachings of Sartum say, young scholar," Anchor Fean answered back. "Magic should only be used when given by the gods. Our Lord Sartum has, over the years, given his Anchors gifts to help them in their work."

Layten shuddered at the thought that magic, MAGIC had been used on him. "It's wrong. It's disgustingly wrong. How could you use magic??"

"I am not. I am only acting as a conduit for Sartum." Anchor Fean pointed at his parents. "Ask them. They know the truth if you will not listen to me."

"Layten, just listen. He's telling the truth. Anchors can do certain things if they need to, to help them in their work." His father looked down at the ground. "We only hid your memories from you to spare you from this reaction."

"Spare me?" Layten still felt ill. "I was excited to leave this place, but still felt guilty leaving my family behind. Now I wish to be gone from here. I'll travel with this Anchor if I must, but do not expect to hear from me anytime soon."

He turned his back on them and could feel fingertips brush his back as he walked away. They were his mother's, he was sure. But the betrayal they had done to him. Allowing him, no, offering him to be touched by that foul force. How could they do this to him! Magic existed, out there. Past the warding circle, the boundaries of good people. Disturbing things, flitters and the water crags and voices, the faint voices that tried to entice fools and drunkards out in the marshes where they were never seen again.

He'd known that, accepted it. But, knowing that he'd been touched by the power itself made his skin crawl. What the Anchor had said was correct. To Layten it had always been a splitting of hairs though. If magic was wrong, evil, then why could the gods use it? The High Prophet Jinir had used magic and renounced it in his conversion to the true faith.

"You are too harsh on them." The voice of the Anchor came from behind him. He hadn't even heard the man get near. "Do you know why Sartum gives us this power? To erase or change memories?"

"No." Layten didn't want to look at the Anchor. It was obvious there was still more he didn't know about here. How his parents knew this person for one. But in the last hour he'd had a lot of things he was sure of challenged, and he wasn't sure he could take anymore.

"Look at me, Layten," the Anchor ordered.

Layten hesitated, but only for a moment. This was still an Anchor. A chosen sacrifice of Sartum. Layten turned to face the Anchor. "Yes?"

"Good. You may be stubborn, but you still have the sense to listen." Anchor Fean nodded. "We are given this power, to help those touched by magic. When someone falls prey to that insidious force, and we rescue them from it, we are able to change their memories to erase that trauma. In your case…." The Anchor paused as if considering things.

"In your case, it became obvious that the warding circle bothered you. It does, doesn't it? Tell me, do you hear a scream? As if someone were in pain?" The Anchor folded his arms together waiting for an answer.

Layten looked at those crossed arms, watching the faint red that still was trying to make its way through the recent bandaging. He didn't want to answer. He'd mentioned it once to his parents a very long time ago. He'd been six or seven. He could remember their shocked reaction now. That was a memory that had been locked away from him.

"Yes," Layten finally answered, his voice barely above a whisper. He cleared his throat. "Yes," he answered again, louder this time.

"It affects some people that way. Certain people. For your safety, it was decided to hide your memories of each warding ritual. That ritual wasn't magic, Layten Grayread. It was a blessing of Sartum." The Anchor unfolded his arms, and poked Layten in the chest. "Your parents actually asked it not to be done. They did not want that for you."

"That doesn't matter. They went along." Layten didn't want to hear this. None of it. "When will we be leaving, Anchor Fean?"

The Anchor said nothing, then turned away. "Go and gather your things. We leave as soon as you are ready."

Everything was already packed; he'd packed it two days ago and checked it and rechecked it more times than he could count. Shouldering his pack, he felt conflicted. He should be excited, happy. He was about to finally leave the drab and wet marsh and become a scholar. It had been all he had ever wanted for years. And yet, he was leaving his parents, his home, and not under good conditions. He wanted to say goodbye. He wanted to make promises that he would come home after his first year to visit during the celebration of the fall. He wanted to.

But he couldn't help but think about his parents letting them erase his memories. The Anchor said they didn't want it to be done. But it had still been done. Could his parents, either of them, have stopped an Anchor? He only had the Anchor's word that they had wanted to stop it. They hadn't said that.

He left the house, giving it all one last look. The low house, facing the reed beds in the marsh. The workshop, twice again the size of the house, full of racks of drying paper. A few workers could be seen moving around. The Anchor and the two Protectors were already on their horses. His parents… were not in sight. His mouth tightened. If they had stayed to say goodbye, he might have said it back.

"They didn't think you wanted to see them." The Anchor spoke. "Come." Layten realized that one thing was different. His horse was there, but... the old warding circle, the one that had been there before was gone. And he saw nothing where it had been. He was curious, but anything to do with the insanity that had been on display before was nothing he wanted to be involved with.

"Come." The Anchor turned his horse and started back down the cart track. The two Protectors followed, their horses' hooves leaving imprints on the soft, damp dirt. It was time.

Chapter Four

Layten took two looks behind him as they moved away from his childhood home. The first time he saw no one, just the sun shining, the morning mists finally being burned away, and of course that warding circle, hanging over the whole place. The second, he could barely make it out, but he thought he saw two figures standing there, watching them disappear past the first turn in the track. Then, there was nothing but trees, and small pools of water.

This part of the trip was safe, or at least usually was. While no one else lived out here, this section of road was in between the smaller warding that protected where he had lived, and the much larger warding that protected the village. As a result, it was usually safe. Which meant, that here, you would see people out and doing whatever. The occasional hunter, or someone foraging for berries, mushrooms, or other less savory items that grew in the damp warm environment. Not that it was completely safe.

A few years back a flock of silverbirds had descended on this patch of forest. They looked like normal birds at first, if normal birds were made entirely of metal, with silver feathers, copper beaks and feet, and gemstone eyes. Of course, that had brought an idiot or two from the village. Instead of leaving them well enough alone until an Anchor could come to deal with it, a few younger men from the village thought they could get rich.

Full of more drink and bravado than sense, they had managed to capture and kill one silverbird based on the one body the searchers found the next day. Which brought the flock down on them. Their bodies were found utterly destroyed, full of small holes and shallow cuts. The Anchor had shown up the next day and did whatever Anchors did, and the flock had vanished. Layten had heard that a few people had gone out trying to find any fallen feathers and the like, but never found anything.

Still, it was safe enough normally. And for Layten it was even safer. He was traveling with an Anchor. And while that was safety, it didn't make him feel much better. He pushed his feelings of betrayal aside and considered how to deal with the village. Being seen in the company of an Anchor wasn't exactly a good thing. The Protectors would be fine. They had to, and everyone knew they dealt with the Anchors if they went mad suddenly. But Layten was known. Why would he be with an Anchor? It wasn't like his family was loved in the village. The Grayread family was tolerated, mostly because they had more income than almost anyone else, and merchants like money. But there were always the whispers about the family living out on the edge of the marsh. There wasn't a great deal going on in the place, so gossip filled the idle time, and Layten's family was a subject of conversation, often.

"What is this village even called?" Protector Binin asked looking back at Layten. "It is marked on the map, but no name was written on it."

"Pol," Layten answered, navigating Gumshoe around a small pothole. "But I don't think many actually know that. It's just 'the village' to most here. It's the only one in miles."

"Why is it here in the first place?" Protector Wilk joined in. "I mean, I understand why your family is where it is. Closer to the raw materials. That makes sense. But the village is just a bunch of poor people living on a crossroads in the middle of nowhere. It's not as if there's a large amount of trade here. And it was here long before your family was."

"I don't know." Layten said, being truthful. "I've never asked."

"You should ask." The Anchor finally spoke. "Not going to be much of a Scholar without being curious. But as it is, I know the answer to that question."

Layten didn't care much for the Anchor already. That comment just made him like the man even less. Still, he couldn't help but be curious. "Well?" Layten waited for the Anchor to share the information.

"Pol exists because at one time it was the main crossroad in what was then Weseg. During the Reunification, when the North was shown the power of Sartum, Pol was the location of the main encampment of the Hammer of Sartum. After the Reunification, it managed to stay around as a village. Barely. I honestly think if your parents had not moved there and set up the business on the marsh coast, the place would now be nothing but weeds and slowly rotting wood." Anchor Fean gave what sounded like a snort, or a chuckle at the end.

Layten wasn't sure if that was the madness in the man, or a sign of how little he thought of the village. If what the man said was true, it was interesting. Layten knew a little about the Reunification. After the destruction of the evil in the south, and the betrayal of the North and the Great God Sartum by the apostates William and Myriam, Sartum had returned to the clean lands in a wrath. He had taken his forces and started a war that reforged the lands of the North into what they are today.

Strong, proud, and free of the evils of magic. A bastion of truth against the evil seductive nature of magical power. A land where humans and later, Gorom, could be free, and not live with the taint given to the world of Alos by the apostates.

Layten had a hard time picturing the village as the main encampment for an army though. The idea of the place being busy and lively was frankly impossible. He'd heard that THREE traders had been in town at the same time once, and that had been the talk of the place for years afterward.

"Interesting." Protector Wilk finally spoke and shrugged, taking his horse into a faster trot. "We aren't too far from Pol. Are we staying the night or moving on, Anchor Fean?"

Layten's chest tightened at the thought of staying the night there. It would be bad enough if people saw him even riding with the Anchor. But staying the night there with him? He didn't plan on coming back here, but even still, that could make for unpleasant conversations for his parents.

"We move on," Fean answered. "The day is young, and the sooner we get Layten to the House of Knowledge, the sooner we can return to Ture."

Both Protectors gave slight head bows at this. Protector Wilk took the lead, and the other one, Protector Binin, took the rear. But Layten noticed both loosened the short riding swords they wore, and Binin also pulled a short spear from the place where it was strapped to the side of her horse. Were they expecting trouble here? In the Village? No one would bother an Anchor. That would be madness. Even if they were hated and feared. To stand in the way of an Anchor would bring the might of the Church of Sartum down on whomever it was, and at dizzying speed. Layten had only ever read of a single event himself in a set of books his parents bought him for a birthday when younger. His father had done it mostly to show him how poor most paper was. It had been right after he'd announced his intention to be a scholar, and his father had still been trying to change his mind.

The account said that roughly two hundred years after the end of the Reunification, a small town by the border to the south, its name now stricken from all records, had taken the Anchor, and drowned him. They renounced the free lands and their ways and claimed to be part of some heathen southern country, and that magic was welcome.

In two days, an Army of nearly twenty thousand armed soldiers of the Hammer of Sartum appeared at the borders of the town. The town, fearing the attack, asked for mercy, and repented. The Hammer had stormed the place and drowned each and every living person and burned the town to the ground. No one ever bothered an Anchor afterward.

"There's no way anyone in the village would ever do something like that," Layten offered. "It's not like that."

"Oh? You know even less than I thought you did, young Layten. But be that as it may… you will take the hooded cloak that Binin will give you and put it on. You will hide your face and features until we are out of the village, and I tell you to remove it, do you understand?" Anchor Fean waved a hand up and Protector Binin appeared by Layten's side offering him a rough and new hooded cloak.

"Why?" Layten asked before catching himself. He had told his parents he would do what the Anchor said while he traveled with him. And as much as he still felt betrayed by them, he wasn't ready to go against their wishes, not in this at least.

"Do it." Anchor Fean said again, with a tone sharp and bitter. Layten felt himself break out into a slight cool sweat, and took the cloak, managing to cover up fairly well before the village came into sight.

Chapter Five

Layten was struck almost at once by how quiet it was. If he came to the village with his parents, or as he got older on the rare occasion by himself, something his mother hated, it had never been like this. While he and his family were thought of as 'odd' by most here, they were also respected some. They had money, and their work at the marsh brought in most of the caravans and traders to this area. If not for the Grayread family, the last of Pol might vanish.

He was expecting to see someone, anyone. He wasn't exactly close to people his age here, what few there were, but he wasn't shunned, or bullied. They all thought him odd, and he found them all silly. He was on speaking terms with the lone innkeeper's son, Havax. And the workers all came back to the village after the season was over. Old Terip lived here, who had been his father's first assistant.

But now, it was that heavy silence that clung to everything. Had something happened to the people? Layten twisted in the saddle wondering what could happen to wipe out a village. But the warding circle was still here. They had passed into its range a while back; the feeling of disconnect then refocus, one he was used to. So, it couldn't be magic. But bandits? Here?

"They hide," Protector Binin whispered. "Look, that window, we are being watched."

Layten tried to follow her nod, and saw a figure move out of sight. An unexpected rush of relief hit him, though he remained confused. "But why? They've seen Anchors before."

"Reasons," Binin answered with a smile. "It's not my place to say."

It didn't make sense. Why hide? Anchors were feared, but this was strange. "I don't understand."

"You don't need to understand. At least not right now. Keep your hood on and lower your head. Once we are out of the village you may remove it." Anchor Fean spoke, his voice clear. "Say nothing else."

Layten wanted to argue but remembered once more the promise he had made and held his retort. He could see it now, figures moving by windows, a pale face watching them through the upper window of an older building. He couldn't make out who it was; the old glass rather dirty and somewhat distorted anyway.

He had hoped they would stop, get some provisions for the road, and then leave. He might miss this place. As it was. Just because it was familiar. Strange, the feeling of familiar. He never loved the place, but realizing he may never see it again made him want to stop, to soak it in. Maybe have mushroom stew that Master Hul made twice a week. But they kept going, the horse's hooves making a thunk as they stepped across partially rotten logs that showed the main track through the place.

The logs gave way once more to a sandy dirt, and the village faded away behind him. Layten still didn't understand the reaction of those who lived there. The Anchor and the Protectors knew more, but they didn't share it, for reasons that made no sense to him.

Layten kept his thoughts to himself. The trip to the House of Knowledge would take two weeks. He could handle this strange Anchor and the Protectors for two weeks. Just keep your head down, don't annoy anyone and do what they say, right? Two weeks wasn't that long of a time. He'd been after this goal for years. He wasn't going to throw it away now because they wouldn't answer questions.

They rode on in relative silence for a while, though Layten wasn't quite sure how long. Long enough that the hood was starting to get warm at least. The air felt different as well, as they moved away from the marshlands, it was drier, and it all smelled different.

"You can take the hood off now," Anchor Fean finally said. Layten removed it with gratitude, though he noticed that the Anchor kept his on still.

"Glad to be away from that marsh," Protector Wilk called back. "Fresher air is always good."

"There's nothing wrong with the marsh air," Layten yelled back. He'd heard that once or twice from trader wagons taking his father's work to the House of Knowledge and the other places that used it.

"You're used to it. I mean no disrespect, but it's too thick, and it smells of dead things," Wilk yelled back again.

Layten frowned. It was a marsh, what did he expect? It was home, and he didn't like anyone poking at it, even now. He tried to think of a way to show that without sounding like a petulant child, but in the end gave up.

"Don't worry about it. Wilk doesn't like anyplace that isn't Ture." Protector Binin kept her voice low. "Though I do agree that it does have its own... odor."

Layten didn't answer. He felt the sliding sensation of leaving the warding circle, and knew they were now technically in unprotected lands. Still, he was with an Anchor. And even if it was outside of the warding circles, this was still land where the Anchor protected them all from the taint of magic.

Layten found himself trying to remember and organize everything he knew about how he could protect himself from that force. He knew magic needed time to grow, to root. While some magical creatures could appear outside of the circles, regardless of what Anchors did, raw magic wasn't able to, at least not often. And if it did, Anchors would absorb it, or something.

But they were on a well-used road, there shouldn't be any issues. It was safe here. He'd never heard of any issues or problems at least. "Protector Binin, where are we going from here? I've never actually been any farther than the village. I've seen maps of course, but…"

"Well, for the next three days and nights we will be on this road. On the fourth, we should make it to Giller. It's a larger trading town. After Giller, we will head north. I'll leave it to the Anchor to decide which route after that." Protector Binin nodded at Anchor Fean. "I think this is the first time he's left Ture in quite a while."

"What do you mean? He's an Anchor, isn't he supposed to be out doing… Anchor things?" Layten found his curiosity up. Any chance to learn things, even if it was about Anchors.

"Yes, and no. Not all Anchors are equal I suppose. A few more… powerful of that order mostly stay in Ture and do whatever it is they do. Protectors live in the Anchorhold. Anchor Fean is usually in the Anchorhold." Protector Binin kept her voice low, giving more than one glance at Anchor Fean's back.

"But why would he leave? Just for this?" Layten hated
this problem. It had been obvious that this Anchor knew
his parents. And somehow knew him. And it was
obvious that he knew of Pol, and its people. He'd done
or said something that kept them away when they had
gone through earlier.

They rode in silence for a while, as the problem gnawed
at Layten. None of it made sense. And the only person
who could give him any clarity on the issue was riding
in front of him, head down. "Anchor Fean?" Layten
finally tried to get the Anchor's attention. His attempt
failed however as the Anchor rode on in silence.

"He won't answer you. You don't want to disturb him
right now anyway. Wait till we stop." Protector Binin's
voice came from behind.

He decided to heed her advice, though it just made yet
another question to ask. It didn't appear that the Anchor
was doing anything, other than riding. His horse didn't
seem to need any direction, and if Layten didn't know
better, he'd have thought that the Anchor was asleep
sitting up in the saddle. But that was impossible.

And they rode on, passing by the occasional clearing,
but usually forest. There wasn't much on this side of
Lowter. Even the clearings were just places the forest
had been cleared for lumber and allowed to regrow. No
buildings or signs of people were to be seen.

They didn't even stop for lunch, a fact that made
Layten less enthused about this trip. He was hot, bored,
and hungry by the time the Anchor suddenly raised his
head. "We stop at the next clearing for the night."

Protector Wilk who had led the trip so far simply nodded from what Layten could see and rode on. Not long after, a clearing came into sight, and Layten was glad to see it. An area of land had been cleared at some point in the last few years, though how long ago Layten didn't know. There was a scattering of new trees growing here and there, but none much taller than the workshop back home. A few bushes, vines, and even a few wildflowers dotted the clearing.

"This will do." The Anchor took his horse into the clearing and, to Layten's eye, seemed to nearly slide off the horse, landing lightly. The Anchor then, however, stumbled a few steps, only to be caught and stopped from falling by the quick action of Protector Wilk, who nearly leapt off his horse to help.

"Thank you, Wilk. It's been a number of years since I've… had to deal with this." The Anchor steadied himself and nodded to Wilk to let go. Layten and Binin dismounted as well, and Binin went straight to Wilk as the two of them spoke in a low tone in a language that Layten had never heard before.

The Anchor, however, was even more a question than whatever they were speaking, as Layten could now clearly see that both hands and wrists were bandaged now, and fresh blood was on both of the wraps. This did not make sense. When they had left, it had only been one, and now both? All the Anchor had done was ride a horse. How had he gotten hurt?

Chapter Six

Layten was going to have to get some answers, somehow. The questions worried at him. He didn't like problems he couldn't solve. It was a part of the reason the House of Knowledge had been his goal. He loved knowing. Not to use it to be better than anyone, or to rule over them. No, he loved knowledge itself. And the questions had built up too much. He thought he'd be able to push this all out of his mind for the trip, but now he knew, that would be impossible.

The Protectors, Wilk and Binin, made the camp ready for the night. A decent-sized clearing was selected, and a shelter put up with a large canvas and leather cover over a small bent-over tree. It was rustic, but acceptable. Rations were pulled out, and while he'd have far preferred something hot, the dry bread and even drier fruit were edible and not bad tasting, though it made his thirst greater. There was enough water until they got to the next location of civilization, but to Layten's mind, it was only barely adequate.

"Ask then." The Anchor finally spoke to Layten directly, the hood ever-present. "I can feel your mind worrying over the questions in your heart from here, Layten Grayread."

Layten almost held his tongue, if only to show his irritation at being discovered this way, by this man. But his thirst for knowing won out. "Who are you? How do you know my parents? What did you say to the village that made them all stay inside? What happened to your arms and hands? You vanished after the warding circle…hanging, and you came back bandaged. And today, all you did was ride a horse, and yet now both arms and hands are bandaged."

"So many questions." Protector Wilk's voice was obviously amused. "More questions that I am not sure you want to know the answers to."

"Silence, Wilk." The Anchor's voice was whip-sharp, and Protector Wilk lowered his head and said nothing more.

"I will answer some of the questions. But not all." Anchor Fean paused. "The village, meaning Pol, I simply told them all to keep watch, and to make sure everyone stayed inside when we passed through. I did not want questions thrown your way or my way if they saw you traveling with me."

"Why would they ask questions?" Layten pushed for more information.

The Anchor ignored the follow-up and continued. "As for the bandages, and good observation I might add, they have to do with being an Anchor. Part of the sacrifice we make to be who we are." Anchor Fean held up his arms slightly. "Pain helps us focus. It keeps the madness away, at least while we are out in the world. I have not had to do this in quite some time. I am rarely out of the Anchorhold."

Layten felt his blood leave his face, and his stomach churn at the same time. They hurt themselves?? Disgust and pity filled him for the Anchor. Hated for what they are, but loved for what they do, the fact that pain held the madness back just made it all that much worse.

"And my parents?" Layten asked again.

"I said I would answer some of the questions, not all." Anchor Fean turned away from Layten and entered the makeshift tent. "Wilk, you take first watch, Binin second. Layten, you will sleep out under the stars." Layten hadn't expected that. Had he done something wrong? Why would the Anchor want him to sleep outside the tent? "Anchor Fean, I don't know if I feel comfortable doing that."

"I did not ask." Anchor Fean's voice was the same whip-sharp tone he used when he was annoyed, or at least done with the conversation. He'd used that tone a few times with the Protectors now, and they had obeyed, instantly. But Layten wasn't a Protector. Protector Binin leaned close. "Do not argue, Layten Grayread. Please?" Her voice was low, nearly a whisper, but the 'not' was clear and strong. Layten remembered he had promised to listen to the Anchor on this trip. He hated it, but he had to. At least he had answers to some of his questions, but the first one still bothered him. And the idea that he didn't want anyone to see him traveling with the Anchor in the village. Yet Layten finally nodded, and he could see some of the tension leave Binin. The Anchor had already entered the tent structure, and was soon followed by Protector Binin, much to Layten's annoyance. The small fire was not much company, and Protector Wilk was not nearly as friendly as Binin. Which left Layten alone with his thoughts.

After a while boredom set in. He'd make notes about everything, and the questions he still had, but it was just too dark to write. The very small campfire didn't help all that much. And while it was a clear night, the moons were not full. Zet was half full, but Lor was only a quarter. The stars were nice to look at though. So, Layten decided to spend some time just staring at them. Making out what constellations that he knew, which wasn't many, and making up ones.

"You should not ask so many questions." Protector Wilk broke the silence.

Layten's mouth twitched in annoyance. He had just finally figured out where the fisher's boat was in the sky when Wilk had spoken, and now he'd lost it again. "I'm going to be a scholar; questions are part of that."

"You think you are going to be a scholar. What you will really be is a scribe. Copying books and manuscripts, written by other people long ago, that have no bearing on anything today." Protector Wilk snorted and poked the small flame of the campfire, drawing new life to its brightness.

"What do you know of it?" Layten worked hard to keep his tone civil. He'd heard this argument before. A few people in the village who knew he was leaving had said similar things. They had been meaner than the Protector though. Layten had learned to brush it off. Most of them couldn't even read. They didn't understand.

"I've been to the House of Knowledge. I see young men and women enter those halls, and leave hunched over from several years of copying texts. I have seen the thirst for knowledge snuffed out, and the bitter anger that replaces it." Protector Wilk shrugged.

"You don't know that." Layten threw back at the Protector. He was sure those scribes were only those who couldn't do well enough to become true scholars. He had the talent and the skill. He would be more than a mindless copier.

"I do. Though, if I understand it correctly, you may have a better time of it. Your father's work may allow you to bypass the fate of most who enter those halls. Maybe." Protector Wilk shook his head. "Not the life I'd want."

"You would rather be a nursemaid to an Anchor?" Layten snapped back, the insinuation that the only thing special about him was his father's work had made him angry. He regretted the words as soon as they had left his mouth, but it was too late to pull them back. He braced himself for the anger that was sure to come his way.

"Layten Grayread, you know nothing about Protectors and Anchors. Don't be a fool." Protector Wilk pointed the glowing end of the stick he'd been poking the fire with at Layten's head. "Forget I said anything, you will see the truth soon enough."

Layten was glad for the dark, that way Wilk could not see the flush in his cheeks as he let his shame free. He'd always been too quick to anger, even more so when people disparaged his dreams and goals. But as much as he disliked the thought, the Protector was right, he did know nothing about the dynamic between an Anchor and his Protectors.

He wanted to ask, but he didn't think Wilk would be rather forthcoming, not now. He could wait for Binin, she seemed friendlier than Wilk anyway. But that would be late at night, and he did need to get some rest. He would be better served to just relieve himself and go to sleep and wait for a better time.

Layten stood, brushing a few loose leaves and old bark off his pants leg. "I will be right back."

"Don't go too far. This isn't well-settled territory; you don't know what's out in the woods." Wilk didn't look at him and didn't ask why he was going anywhere.

Layten picked a careful path towards the nearest tree line, in an attempt at a small amount of modesty. He almost stepped into some animal burrow and was glad he spied it. Breaking an ankle or twisting a knee would not make for a pleasant trip. He wouldn't be surprised if that happened that they wouldn't just turn around and dump him back at home. He was sure Protector Wilk might enjoy that.

It didn't take long for him to reach his destination. A strand of silver-barked pin needle trees with a single red birch in the middle. Something about it bothered Layten, but it wasn't the time. He quickly did his business when the realization hit him. This wasn't natural. The pin needles were planted in a perfect circle around the red birch.

Why would someone plant this? Had something else been here once? Some long-forgotten outposts, maybe a family burial plot to some vanished farm? The ground was clean under the red birch, clean and debris-free. That was odder still. That meant this wasn't abandoned. Someone was tending this. Or something…

Layten stumbled back, the implications that something involving magic might be going on here scared him. He had to get back to the Anchor. He'd be safe there. He had to. He must! He spun around trying to make a run, and slammed his head into a branch, falling to the ground grasping the place where he'd been hit.

Pain coursed through him, and shock. There had not been any branches that low before. He was sure of it. He KNEW it. He tried to stand, his head throbbing making it hard to focus, only to find that somehow branches and a vine had gotten tangled in his shirt and legs. The fear turned to terror. What was going on? He thrashed about, trying to free himself, but every time he moved, something else seemed to catch or trip him. He opened his mouth to yell for help, when a large clod of dirt and leaves was thrown into it, forcing him to choke and spit, unable to get a word out.

"Look, a HUUUMAN." A soft voice came, and a tinkling of bells.

Chapter Seven

Layten struggled to see where the voice came from, his stomach tying itself in knots. This was magic. MAGIC. He felt unclean, dirty. His stomach churned at the thought of even being exposed to things like this. Did he ever really want to see what had spoken? And how could anything like this be so close by and the Anchor not know about it?

"He struggles, the human does." The voice came again, whisper-thin, more like the steps of a cat stalking its prey than any real sound.

"Fool. Why capture it? The lost one isn't that far away. If that one comes here, you will die." A second voice, high-pitched and fast-spoken, though Layten could make it out if he tried.

"I knew that. It didn't matter. The moment this one saw the pattern, my life here was over." The first voice spoke again, full of sorrow. Layten, for a moment, had a mental image of falling dead leaves, of a tree rotting, a deep sorrow.

"Bffffttt. He's a human, he'd make something up and not mention it. Now he will. The lost one will come for sure now." The high-pitched voice seemed closer somehow, louder, though neither voice was loud in a normal sense.

"Don't kill me." Layten managed to force the words out, having finally cleared enough of the dirt and leaves out from before. The knot of fear and disgust grew in him.

"Oh, he speaks." The high-pitched voice added what Layten could only think was scorn to his words. "Humans make no sense."

"Not all humans are bad, Fingolden. In the south…." The first voice spoke again, a sorrowful tone.

"Yes. Yes. In the south. But we aren't in the south. We are in the realm of IT. The destroyer, the glutton that never is full. Of the thing and its kin that want to feast until this world is lost." The high-pitched voice threw the words out, the venom in them plain even with the tone and speed with which they were said.

Layten struggled to follow. Who was the destroyer? He didn't get it. What was a lost one? "I don't understand. Please. I just want to leave." He finally managed to turn his head enough to see the speakers, which didn't make his fear any less.

One of the voices belonged to what Layten could only describe as a ghost. It was small though, a pale green to golden color, with the occasional flash of dark green. It hovered near the red birch, attached to it, joined with it. The other voice was something Layten had heard of at least, but he'd prayed he'd never see. A Flitter. This creature, less than a foot high, wearing clothes of brown and grey, stared at him with a grim face, an angry face.

"Well, human. You see us now." The Flitter pulled a tiny needle-looking weapon from his side. The pale green light that the other thing gave off barely reflected enough of the thing for it to be seen. "I should stab your eyes out with this."

"Leave him be, Fingolden. You can see his terror." The first thing spoke again.

Layten didn't see how it could talk. There was no face, no form, just a wispy vague thing that was only slightly more solid in the center. "What… what are you?" He couldn't help but ask. He was disgusted and terrified by being this close to anything that had to do with that evil power that is magic, but he was also fascinated by this thing.

Fingolden sneered at Layten. "You reek of fear, of hate. Why should we tell you anything?"

"I am a Holant. A tree spirit. In time I would have been able to make my tree walk and move. In time. Time that I will no longer have, thanks to you." The Holant gave a single pulse of grey and white.

"Let me go, please. Don't kill me. Don't taint me." Layten found himself begging. "I just want to be a scholar. I don't… just don't."

Fingolden approached him, its tiny sword to the ready, when a wave of ice cold seemed to pass over Layten. Its effect was immediate. The Flitter screamed, and dropped its tiny weapon, grasping at its head. The Holant gave a brief whistle, and a large part of its floating form was torn apart, like smoke being blown away by the wind.

Layten felt the icy touch as well, but it brought him more confusion than anything else. A confusion that was short-lived. He heard the running footsteps and knew; his companions had come. The Flitter scowled and with one last hissing scream vanished. A slight hint of blue light seemed to flash in front of Layten. A sight that made his already frayed nerves on edge. Every child in the North knows the signs of magic.

The other thing, the Holant, having already been damaged by whatever had happened before was slowly falling apart, not making a sound as it did so. A small, tiny part of Layten felt somewhat sorry for the creature, but he pushed that thought away. It was wrong, and the Anchor would set things right.

The two protectors burst into the clearing, weapons drawn, hacking at branches, and clearing a path. Protector Binin moved forward and cut Layten free, helping him to his feet. The moonlight, such as it was, lit the clearing with a pale silver-white glow, as the Holant faded even more.

The Anchor came next, a grasping cold coming from him in waves. Layten shivered as an image of a great yawning chasm seemed to move into his mind as he watched Anchor Fean raise his staff and mutter something, slam it into the ground, and hold onto the black oily surface of the thing as if it could save him from being pulled away.

There came a rushing of wind, as everything was pulled towards the staff and the Anchor. The final remnants of the Holant disintegrated in front of Layten, pulled into the staff. A mournful echo came to Layten as it did so, but he dismissed it as just the rushing wind passing by his ears.

The trees around him in the tiny circle bowed toward the staff, and they began to change as well. The color and life left them, leaves grew thin, and pale, reflecting the moonlight in a white halo that would have been almost pretty, if it hadn't been accompanied by the sudden stench of death and decay.

The smell was strong, and Layten struggled not to retch his meager meal from earlier onto the ground. Each of the pin needles died first, and then, finally the red birch, its skin now stark white, its leaves gone, stood alone, dead. It was only then that Anchor Fean pulled the staff up with a shuddering intake of breath.

"See… to... our companion, Binin. I must… go."
Anchor Fean's voice was not like any other time Layten
had heard him speak. Each word was clipped, as if he
were holding something back, some overwhelming
feeling. It was then he remembered, *An Anchor must
hurt himself, or go mad.*
Anchor Fean half stumbled, half ran towards the
direction of the tent, followed by Wilk. Layten
shuddered at the thought of all magic, having to touch
it, dispose of it. "Will he be, ok?"
"I hope so." Protector Binin shook her head. "How did
this happen? Why did you wander into the woods?"
"I had to…." Layten felt awkward telling her why he
had come.
"It's not all your fault. This isn't the first time I've
heard of this happening. The south and its pollution is
spreading to the free lands more and more." Protector
Binin touched the dead red birch with an outstretched
finger for a second. "This will not go over well at the
Anchorhold."
"This happens often now? What do you mean?" Layten
didn't even want to look at the trees. The south was
pushing North? What did she mean?
"I have been a Protector for many years. In the last
three years I've heard of this kind of thing happening
often enough to make me worry." Protector Binin
shook her head. Layten watched in disgust as the
Protector pushed her finger into the tree, its now white
bark giving way to nothingness as the tree began to
crumble into dust. "See, without the illusion of life
given to it by magic, it's nothing. It was never a real
tree."
"Can we go now?" Layten stepped back from the still
crumbling thing, suddenly afraid of inhaling the dust
and what it might do to him.

"Yes. But, from now on, stay away from the forest."
Protector Binin led Layten away. "Once the Anchor
has… found himself again, he will want to know
exactly what happened, every detail. I trust as a future
scholar you remember the events clearly. Do not lie to
him."

Layten shuddered at the memories, but he knew he'd
not forget. And Protector Binin was correct. As a future
scholar he had to be truthful and honest, or what was
the point? Yet even as he worked to remember the
details, it all grew a little vague in his mind, as if some
part of him was actively trying to forget the whole
thing.

He concentrated trying to remember each word said,
where he had been, what he had done. He carefully
stepped over a few of those burrows and avoided some
bush that seemed to be more thorn than leaves as he
committed everything that had happened to memory.
The vague feeling of dullness faded, but a new and
even more strange feeling overtook him. The Holant.
Remembering the thin ethereal creature brought sadness
and pain. It was a magical creature. By its very nature it
was evil, wrong. It should never have been. Yet, it had
been gentle, it hadn't wanted to hurt him. It had just
wanted to exist. To live.

Was that so wrong? To simply wish to live wasn't a bad
thing, it wasn't wrong. Was it? Layten stumbled and
nearly fell as he realized where his thoughts had taken
him. No! It had to be evil. This was why magic was
forbidden to mortals. It was insidious, exploited our
weaknesses, our kindness, our good natures.

Back in their small camp the only sound that came was the crackling of the fire. Binin stood by the small flame, not looking at Layten at all. Her eyes were locked onto the small tent space, from which the only sound was silence. Layten did find that strange, to go along with all the other oddities he'd been exposed to as of late. He thought again about what had happened at the trees. He had calmed down now, but he realized he had another question for the Anchor. Why had he never seen the man's face? In fact, thinking about all the other Anchors he'd seen, now that his memories were back, he never had seen any Anchor's faces. The more he thought about it, the more it bothered him. He hadn't considered it much, at least before. But in replaying the night, he had realized the hood ALWAYS covered the Anchor's face. Even when he had jumped into the clearing and wielded that horrid staff of his. The hood had moved, but still, it always covered his features. "How long do you think I will need to wait? Should I try to rest?" Layten looked up at the stars, noting that while the night was still dark, the barest hint of a lightening was gathering in the east, or at least he thought it was east.

"I doubt we will be moving until the next morning, Layten Grayread." Protector Binin nodded her head at the tent. "That… event, was dangerous for him."

"Why?" Layten frowned at the thought. He'd heard stories of Anchors banishing huge numbers of things at once. He hadn't quite believed them, but they had been common enough.

There was a long pause before the Protector answered. "He is… old." Protector Binin shook her head. "None of this is for me to say."

Layten debated pushing her for more answers. He'd get more information from her than Wilk, he was sure. Yet, as his mind calmed after everything, he found himself feeling tired, and his eyes fell. Maybe once he was more awake, he'd get the answers he wanted. Yes, that would be good. Rest now, answers in the morning.

Chapter Eight

"He will keep asking questions you know? He does have the right mind for being a scholar." Protector Binin looked down at the sleeping form of Layten. "He's a good young man. Strong. Most people his age would have had a much harder time of it, with that little encounter in the woods."

"He can ask all he wants, but I will be the only one to answer. Or not answer." Anchor Fean stood on the other side of the fire, wearing his ever-present hood. "Though this trip has cost me more than I ever expected it to."

"You shouldn't have even made this trip." Protector Wilk stood next to Binin, his face pulled into a tight frown. "You should not have left the Anchorhold."

"You mean you didn't want to leave the Anchorhold," Anchor Fean shot back, with a trace of humor in his voice. "It had been too long since I had walked the lands of the North."

"That's not what I mean. If anyone in the Anchorhold ever found out the real reason you did this task, things would go badly for you, very badly. And for us as well." Protector Wilk shook his head. "And you tampered with his memories again, he won't even really remember much from last night, will he?"

"No, he won't. Questions he had, things he remembered, all will be gone. Good idea telling him to remember those things, Binin. It kept it all fresh in his mind, which made it easier to prune." Anchor Fean tapped the ground twice with his staff, the surface of the thing appearing to twist in the flickering light of the fire. "But the matter of those things even being here, that concerns me."

"What if we run into more of those vile outbursts? Can you even take more?" Protector Binin pointed at the staff in the Anchor's hands. "I would prefer not to have to take the descent, and I'm sure you and Wilk feel the same."

"I do not know. If it hadn't been Layten who had stumbled into that foul nest, I don't think I would have taken the power. But by Sartum's will, it was." Anchor Fean shook his head. "Assuming we do get back to the Anchorhold, we will have to discuss these incursions."

"What about Layten then?" Protector Wilk looked at the slumbering form. "Does anything change?"

"No. We take him to the House of Knowledge and leave him there. With any luck, he will stay there and live out the life he wants." Anchor Fean raised a heavily bandaged hand and arm, one with only four fingers now. "And he will be none the wiser."

Layten awoke with a jerk. He'd been dreaming of running through a strange forest. Silver-barked trees and a thin wispy floating thing crying. It didn't make any sense, but he had known he had to escape. He'd been running and then had tripped…. And awoken.

"Good morning." Protector Wilk and Protector Binin stood near the horses, fully dressed in their leather and chain armor. "Stow your gear. I have some dried fruit and bread for you to eat. We will make a strong pace today and try to make it to Giller tonight." Protector Binin held out a chunk of hard travel bread and a small canvas bag that must hold whatever dried fruit she had mentioned.

Layten took them but shook his head. "There is something I was going to ask about, but I can't seem to remember it now. Some scholar I will be if I can't even remember a simple question."

"Just the fog of sleep, I'm sure it will come to you." Protector Wilk waved Layten towards his horse. "Go on, get yourself organized, we are waiting."

Layten realized that the Protector was right. As the last dregs of sleep left him, he saw that the Anchor was already on his horse, and everything was cleaned up. Even the fire was out. Feeling slightly out of sorts and embarrassed by his inaction, Layten quickly gathered his bedroll and other items and stowed them on Gumshoe.

He climbed into the saddle, still feeling oddly unsettled. He'd slept hard last night, he must have. He didn't remember falling asleep, or much from last night at all. Travel must have tired him out more than he'd thought.

"Giller." Layten looked up from where he'd been staring at the saddle. "You said it would take three days to get there, but we can make it tonight now?"

"We aren't going to take the road. Anchor Fean is needed back at the Anchorhold, so we are going to take a shortcut. It goes through the woods and over a small pass between two small mountains." Protector Binin pointed to the northwest.

Layten followed her finger and saw in the distance two old mountains, standing alone. He knew their names. "Holdrian and Gunnor," Layten spoke without thinking. "Named after the two lords of Lowter who joined the side of Sartum in the great war."

"Very good," Anchor Fean finally spoke. "You will make an excellent scholar. Now we must go. Protector Wilk, will you lead the way?"

Layten took his place behind Anchor Fean, followed by Protector Binin again. His mind wasn't on the bread he was eating now, or the dried golden berries. Was it his imagination, or did the Anchor sound weak? Was that a tremor in the Anchor's voice?

The thought was fleeting as the Anchor didn't say another thing as they rode. Protector Wilk led them off the road quickly, and through the woods. Thankfully, at least to Layten, the route wasn't as overgrown as he had been afraid of. The trees here weren't overly close, and he only rarely had to deal with ducking a branch.

In a way this shortcut almost made things go faster for him. On the road Layten had been bored. At least here he was having to pay attention to where he was going and making sure that Gumshoe didn't take a wrong step.

The day passed quickly, the only odd thing being a strange feeling of fear and a hint of nausea when they rode through some pin needle trees. He wasn't sure why. They didn't have them back home, at least not much. Back in the marsh there were similar trees to be sure, but most of them were outside the warding circle, and so, off limits.

But the trees and the unease that came with them passed quickly, and so out of his mind as well. The morning wore on as they slowly climbed upward. Layten wasn't exactly sure what time it was when suddenly Protector Wilk held up a hand to halt.

"Quick stop. Binin, come with me. Layten. Anchor Fean. Please stay right here." Protector Wilk dismounted and pulled a short but deadly-looking blade out. "Do not follow us." Wilk nodded to Binin who had dismounted as well and drawn an equally dangerous-looking blade.

Layten stayed on his horse but found himself almost bursting with curiosity. What had the Protector seen? What was ahead? "What is happening? Why have we stopped?" Layten finally asked the Anchor.

"I am not certain," Anchor Fean answered, but he kept his voice low. "I do not think it overly dangerous, or Wilk would have not left us here. But still, it is strange."

"What is the Anchorhold like?" Layten asked, trying to fill the silence. No one had said he couldn't talk after all. "I don't know much about Anchors."

"Not many do." Anchor Fean shook his hooded head. "But that is for the best. The Anchorhold is in Ture. Built on the remains of the old Smithing Guild there. From the days of the schism."

"Oh." Layten frowned in thought. He knew about the schism. Every good follower of Sartum did. When the enemies of man had managed to attack and cleave the true God into two. Amder and Valnijz. How this corruption of what was supposed to be had caused wars and death for centuries before the false ones had returned the true God to life, only to betray him in his moment of victory.

"What can Anchors do exactly? I still don't understand why my memories were changed back at the workshop." Layten didn't like thinking about it and had tried to ignore that it had even happened. The betrayal by his parents gnawed at him if he let it.

Anchor Fean didn't answer for a minute. Just long enough for Layten to wonder if the man was going to answer at all. The only sound was the horses nosing around for something to eat in the underbrush, the occasional bird, and the buzzing of a few flies who had discovered the mobile feast of the horses.

"I will not speak of this again. Your parents decided to take that step to protect you from the memories of seeing the circle being activated. That is all." Anchor Fean sat up in the saddle. "They return."

Layten didn't like the answer at all. It didn't make sense to him. Why did he need to be protected? He found the whole thing rather disturbing, but he needed to know the truth, right? But the Protectors were back, so he let it go, for now.

Both Protectors had put their weapons away, so that was a good sign. "What was it?" Layten asked before the Anchor could speak. Instantly he realized he'd probably overstepped his bounds, but the words were already out there.

"Abandoned cabin, probably a hunter or woodcutters. We needed to make sure there weren't any… surprises there. Empty though. Been empty for a while by all appearances." Protector Binin remounted her horse, followed by Protector Wilk.

"Come, we wasted too much time on this as it is." Protector Wilk took the lead once more, and the long ride continued.

Layten soon saw the cabin in question. How the Protector had even spotted it was a mystery to him. There was no way to see it from where they had been. The place was strange though. It made him cold, his skin breaking into small bumps as they rode past. And it became oddly quiet in these woods near the building. The birds were distant, and even the sounds of the wind through the leaves were muted.

"Everything alright?" Protector Binin asked from behind him.

Layten stilled himself in his saddle. He had been shifting too much at the feeling. "Yes, just trying to get comfortable. Not used to riding this much." The words slid out with no thought to them. Layten almost frowned. Why had he lied?

Chapter Nine

The cabin faded behind them, and the cold tingle left Layten as it did so. The woods seemed normal again. He soon found himself distracted once more by the navigation through the woods. The trees became sparser here, and the ground rockier. Despite the fact they hadn't stopped for lunch, he did find this trip somewhat enjoyable.

He really hadn't been many places. He'd read about as many as he could and spoke to the traders and caravan masters who had stopped to take his father's wares to Ture and beyond. But there was no trading reading about something for seeing it himself. He knew there was a small pass between these mountains. But he'd never seen it. He'd only seen a map once from a wagon driver who had been bored enough and amused by a young Layten's pestering to show him.

The only downside to seeing it all was that now that they were in a much more open part of the shortcut, there was much less to distract his mind, and he began to grow bored again. Talking to Wilk was out of the question, and the Anchor never seemed all that interested in talking to him. So that left Protector Binin. "Protector Binin, what is Villi like? I saw an etching once, but since you are from there…." Layten left the question open, hoping she'd answer.

"It's been a long time since I was there. Long time. But I remember liking it. The canals were nice. You could take a small boat anywhere in the city for the most part, and if you weren't right there, you could walk the short distance left." Protector Binin's voice rose as she spoke, conjuring an image of a fair city.

Layten could almost see it, before something he'd read
came back to him. "I thought the canals were destroyed
in the great drought?" Layten tried to remember; he'd
read that a long time ago, he was sure of it. There had
been a two-year period where the whole of the eastern
coastline of the North had been in the grips of a terrible
drought nearly fifty years ago.

Many places ended up falling into ruin and being left to
the winds. Villi had survived by using every scrap of
water in the canals to survive. After the drought had
passed, they simply filled the canals up and made them
into roads; it was faster that way, or something.

"Oh. Yes. Sorry, I was... thinking about the past. You
are right of course." Protector Binin paused. "Maybe
that's why I never go back. I prefer to think of how it
must have been." Her tone was one of dismissal.

Layten could tell he'd hit a sore spot, and, not wanting
to antagonize the one person who spoke to him, let it
drop. Still, it was a strange answer from her. Finally,
they rose over a small ridge to see the pass, a trail, not
well-marked, that seemed to split the two mountains in
half.

The trail did not look well-used. Almost all the traders
used the main roads. Safer that way. Out here, there
was the chance of bandits, wild animals attacking the
slower-moving oxen or pack horses. And, of course, the
worst threat, magic.

The only sign that anyone had ever been here was the
ruins of a small watchtower, and a half-wall over by
itself. Layten wondered who had built it all, and when.
Had this route been used often enough to call for it in
the past? He wished the tower could tell him its secrets.
What had it been made for? Who had lived there?
When had it been left to fall apart?

"Come. Giller lies on the other side." Protector Wilk led them through the pass, the sides narrow enough that they had to ride single file now. Layten realized it was later than he'd thought. The sun was already starting to fall behind the edge of the mountain named Gunnor. At least he thought it was Gunnor.

They had spent far longer in that forest than he'd thought they had. The thought made his stomach growl with the realization of just how long ago breakfast had been. Layten didn't complain though, if his companions could ride all day without eating, so could he. He'd had a few sips of water through the day, but he'd not been overly thirsty. He put that down to not having been exposed to the direct sun like he would have been on the road.

They rode on in silence, his comment about Villi having seemed to make Binin shut her mouth tight. Not that this was much of a place for talking. It felt odd, riding through this narrow stone path, carved into the rock of the mountains. The occasional vine clung to the rock desperately trying to keep enough leaves in the sunlight to find its way down here.

They passed a few thin trickles of water that sprang from cracks in the rock. Layten took note of that. If someway or somehow, they got separated, he'd know where some water was. He didn't have any idea if it was safe to drink, but it was at least something. Why was he even thinking that? Letting out a breath he cleared his head. There was nothing wrong; he just was tired and on edge because of it. *Right?*

As the sun set more, the shadows grew even longer, and finally Protector Wilk drew to a halt. "Torches now," was all he said.

Protector Binin behind him pulled two torches from her saddlebags. All he had was extra clothes, pens, and a journal he had sadly not written a single thing in yet. If they did find Giller and stayed there, he'd try to find time to at least make a short list of notes that he could expand on later. He didn't want to forget anything.

Binin offered one to Layten, but he shook his head. His nerves were getting the better of him, though he wasn't sure why.

The torches were lit with a minimum of effort, and they resumed their ride. The torchlight made it more mysterious though. The flickering and moving light threw strange reflections on the walls of the pass. Layten felt a pain in his hand and looked down to see he'd been gripping his hands so tight on the reins that he'd cut into his own palm with his fingernails.

He consciously released his fist, telling himself he was being a fool. He was with an Anchor. And two Protectors. No magical creature was going to come near them with the Anchor here. And no human would want to bother two Protectors. No other race would either, not that those other races were common here.

At last, the darkening shadows around them grew less, and they found the pass widen until they stood on the edge of a path heading down, and at the bottom, a town far larger than anything Layten had ever imagined. He'd sort of imagined what a real town would look like, but this… this was far beyond anything he'd pictured. In his imagination, Giller was two or three times the size of the village. But this was easily ten times or more. It was massive! "How many people LIVE there?" Layten managed to ask, stunned by the sight.

"Giller? Maybe two or three thousand. It's just a small trading town. But it's just large enough to have a harbor for us," Wilk answered quickly. "Shall I, Anchor Fean?"

"Yes. Make sure it's prepared for us. We will see you there." Anchor Fean finally spoke again after hours of silence. His voice was low and lacked any energy. Layten had no idea what they meant by a harbor. Giller was landlocked. There wasn't even a river here. He watched Wilk ride ahead, his torch quickly vanishing as he rode with speed down the path towards the town. Two or three thousand people? And that was small? He'd never seen even a hundred people together in one place. This was going to take some getting used to.

He, Protector Binin, and Anchor Fean continued down the path at a more leisurely rate. This time Protector Binin took the lead, leaving Layten to follow up the rear. A position he didn't like. He kept looking behind him, seeing if anything was there. He was sure that for a second he saw a flash of something, but it was gone so fast he wasn't sure if he'd just imagined it.

Trying to distract himself, Layten fell back into his favorite pastime. Asking questions. "Excuse me, but what did he mean by a harbor? Giller is not a port, there's not even a river or a lake here."

Of all the reactions he could have got, the burst of actual laughter from Anchor Fean wasn't what he'd expected. It wasn't the crazed giggle of an Anchor who was near his end. This was a deep laugh of actual humor. Which made it in some ways just as unnerving as a giggle would have been, coming from the normally stoic Anchor.

"Apparently High Prophet Jinir had a sense of humor about Anchors. Everything dealing with the order has as many nautical terms attached to it as possible. Hence, harbor. A rest and way station for Anchors on the road, and their Protectors." Anchor Fean shook his head. "And guest of course."

"Oh." Layten found himself slightly disappointed with that. He'd wanted to stay in an inn. A real inn. With traders and travelers. Music, drink, and all the like. Instead, he was going to be staying in some strange Anchor way house.

But he was sure most people didn't have any idea what a harbor was like inside, so he could make notes. The idea of being able to describe something like that and have a somewhat unique experience cheered Layten up considerably. And it wasn't like he wasn't ever going to set foot in an inn. He was sure once he was settled in the House of Knowledge, he'd make friends and find himself in many an inn, arguing esoteric facts and showing off for women who wouldn't even think twice about him.

Layten felt his mood improve some the more he thought about it. It was better this way. Going to a busy inn with an Anchor could be a mistake anyway. No, this 'harbor' was probably the best bet. Thankfully the trip down to Giller from the pass was not a hard one. The trail wasn't used that often but showed signs of some use. And even better, that feeling of something behind him had faded as they had left the pass.

Layten was sure it was just his nerves and the excitement of his trip. Some food, and a night hopefully spent sleeping somewhere more comfortable than the ground would suit him fine. Maybe even a bath. He hadn't gone this long without bathing in a while. His mother had always insisted that he and his father bathe every day. She claimed the smell of making the paper clung to them and she wasn't going to have her house smelling that way.

They were within sight of the main gate when Protector Wilk came riding out to meet them, with three other armor-clad riders in livery of green and red. Some kind of city guard? Layten didn't see any sigils; he'd tried to learn most of those found here in Lowter. But it was dark enough that it would be hard to see anyway.

"The harbor is ready for us, Anchor Fean. The city guards sent a… delegation to guide us to our rest." Protector Wilk kept his voice carefully neutral, but to Layten he was sure there was tension in it.

"Well, we wouldn't want to argue with the city leaders, now, would we?' Anchor Fean nodded. "Come Binin, and guest."

"Halt." A guard who was older than the others held up a hand. "What guest?"

"My guest." Anchor Fean sat up more in his saddle than Layten had seen so far. The man practically slouched over all the time, so this was different. "Would you care to argue with me about it?"

The older guard locked eyes with Layten, then dropped his eyes down. "Of course not, Anchor. It's just…" The older guard shook his head. "Come, we will lead the way."

Layten wondered exactly what that was all about. People were afraid of Anchors, but you don't go questioning them. The Church of Sartum would have your head if they got wind of it. Still the guard had backed down quickly enough. And now they were being led inside. Inside a real town.

Chapter Ten

Layten followed the Anchor as Binin took up the rear guard again. Layten noticed that she kept her free hand near her sword. So, she was more on edge here than even during the ride through the woods. To him this was exciting, not dangerous. The gate swung open, revealing more buildings than he had ever seen in one place.

As they passed through the stout timber walls, Layten worked to not look around in stunned awe. Wood and stone buildings, some three stories, were full of people. He didn't see any that were using fatted skin as a poor window, everything had real glass, and well-made glass at that.

Even though it was night, there were more than a few people out and about. A pair of women, smelling of beer, walked by laughing loudly. A cart full of bread and sausage rolled past, the driver calling out his wares and prices. The smell made his stomach do flips, but he didn't have time to stop. The guards were taking them off the main road, and through a series of smaller ones. He pushed Gumshoe to keep up, as they wound through small roads, and even an alley or two. Soon they were in a less open part of the city. Older buildings, some windows broken, and most unlit, were around them now. A few had sounds coming from them, but what sounds they were Layten wasn't sure. Maybe it was better he didn't know.

There was no one but them on the streets here, though they did disturb a cat who was stalking some unseen animal, provoking a hiss and a scamper away from them. Protector Wilk glanced back at the Anchor and shook his head, which made Layten all the more curious as to what he didn't know about this.

Finally, they came around a corner to a large open area. In the exact middle was a single building, decorated with seashell images and bearing a set of jet-black doors that gave Layten a feeling similar to the warding circle back home. That faint echo of a scream and cold. Deep cold. The group pulled up suddenly, distracting him from his feeling.

"We are here. When will the Anchor and his... company be leaving?" The older guard asked, keeping his face turned away from them.

"In the morning, before the tenth bell, I assure you." Anchor Fean answered, his voice as flat as Layten had ever heard it. The Anchor wasn't a man who showed much emotion anyway, but if his voice could have been flatter, Layten wasn't sure how.

The guards moved back and away from the building but watched Layten and the others closely. Protector Wilk headed to the building, this harbor. There was a place to tie up the horses outside at least. Layten dismounted and almost at once felt his legs go weak. He'd not ridden that much ever. He hoped very much that in the morning he'd not be too sore. He had a long way to ride yet.

Anchor Fean approached the door, a singular thing silver and other colors that didn't stand out well in the dim light. This open area wasn't well lit, and the torches that the two Protectors were carrying were already down to nubs by now.

Layten couldn't see what the Anchor was doing, but in a few moments the door swung open, revealing a well-lit interior. The light was almost too bright, and it was the wrong color. The warm reds and yellows of torches or lanterns were replaced with a bright white, almost like sunlight on a clear winter day. Without a word the Anchor and the two Protectors went inside, followed closely by Layten. The door swung closed behind them with a satisfactory click.

"Fools. Arrogant and stupid fools," Protector Wilk said as soon as the door had closed fully. "You should have let me educate them on how to treat an Anchor."

"Let it go, Wilk. They are just afraid." Binin retorted. "Yes, it was rude, but we are here, and we are safe."

"For now." Protector Wilk walked down a short hall and pushed open a more normal-looking door, revealing a small kitchen and eating table. "Food soon. Let's see if they kept their word."

Layten didn't know who he was talking about. Whose word? The guards? They had led them here. But what did that have to do with eating? He wanted to ask, but he was grabbed by the arm by Protector Binin.

"Come Layten, I'll show you where you are bunking down this evening." Protector Binin opened a side door revealing another short hall with four doors, two on each side. She pushed in the second one on the right, revealing a clean room with two bunks. "Here. Protectors can use this room, but we will be in the one in front of Anchor Fean's room."

Protector Binin pointed at the far wall where another door lay. "Past that is a bathing room. On the far side of that room is another door. You are not to even try to open that door, do you understand? It is for Anchors only."

Layten nodded, though his mind immediately went into questions. What was special about that room? Was there only one here, or did each group of rooms have its own? From what The Protector had said, it seemed like there were more of those rooms. But why? Why did the Anchors need their own room?

"Don't ask, Layten Grayread." Protector Binin snapped her fingers breaking his thoughts. "Get cleaned up, and then come back to the kitchen area. A good meal, then rest. But do not open that door. Do not touch that door. Do not even look at it if you can help it. Do you understand, Layten?"

Layten hadn't heard that tone in her voice before, but it was steel-edged and sharp this time. It was that more than the words that made him nod in agreement. Binin smiled and slapped him on the back, making him stumble forward and wince in pain.

"Good! Hurry though. We are all hungry. Take too long and there won't be anything left for you." Protector Binin left, her footsteps fading quickly.

Layten put everything down and disrobed to get bathed. Stepping into the next room, he was happy to see a bathing tub and a clean barrel of water. He didn't see a way to heat it, but he didn't care at this point. Of course, his eyes were drawn to the one place he was told not to look or go.

On the far wall stood a single yellow and silver door. The handle on it was twisted and strange, and he found his arm giving a twitch at the thought of opening the thing. But what bothered him the most was the feeling. That same echoing coldness in his chest. He'd felt it before, but… he couldn't remember where, not all the time. He'd felt it near the cabin they had passed. But he'd felt it elsewhere. He knew that.

The thought of it tried to skitter away, like water falling on a hot pan. Pan. The thought made his stomach growl. Food. He turned away from the door and did his best to put it out of his mind. As quickly as he could, he washed himself of the travel grime and dirt. It was a temporary respite, he knew that. They still had a good amount of travel in front of them, and he wasn't sure how many times they were going to stop.

He dried himself and pulled a mostly clean set of clothes out of his packs. He hoped there was someplace he could go to clean this stuff at some point. He didn't have that many changes with him. And he didn't want to present himself at the House of Knowledge smelling like dirt, sweat, and horse. But those were problems for another day. Right now, the bath and clean clothes had taken care of a lot, but one glaring thing remained. Hunger.

Layten quickly made his way back into the kitchen and eating area and found himself not the last to arrive, thankfully. While the two Protectors were there, the Anchor was nowhere in sight. Wilk hadn't even bathed yet by the looks of things, he'd just started cooking. Binin however had bathed and changed. It was the first time he'd ever seen her not in her armor. She was shockingly younger-looking than he'd expected.

Her hair had a strange sheen to its dark brown, almost red color. He knew it had a name, but he couldn't remember it. No one in the village or his parents' workshop had hair that color, he'd only read about it. She'd made several mentions about how long she'd been a Protector though. It did not add up.

"Food's ready. Here, Binin, take this to the Anchor. I'll serve the rest up here, and we can eat. Then I'll leave the clean-up to you and take my own bath." Protector Wilk pushed a small tray to Binin with a slab of some cheese, a bowl of soup, a large hunk of bread, and a bottle of some greenish liquid.

"The Anchor isn't eating with us?" Layten asked before he realized that to eat, he'd have to see the Anchor's face. And he never saw the man's face. That thought bothered him. He had thought that before, hadn't he? Was it just occurring to him now? No… did he remember asking that? The thought made his head hurt.

"No. The Anchor eats alone." Protector Wilk placed the same food at the table as Layten had seen on the tray, minus the bottle. They were served just plain water. But very cold water at least. The bowl did have soup, bits of vegetables and some meat floated in it. The bread was fresh. He didn't recognize the cheese, but that was another thing there wasn't a lot of back home. On occasion a merchant would be willing to sell or trade his mother some, but only a few times a year. And that stuff had been bright white with a hard blue wax coating it.

This was blinding bright orange. It smelled good though. It all smelled good. Binin reappeared quickly, and they all set to eating. There wasn't any conversation as they all lost themselves in the relief of eating. Layten dunked half his bread in the soup and ate it that way, then drank the soup. Taking a small bite of the cheese, he decided he liked it, and finished that off with the rest of the bread.

In short order Layten leaned back some from the table, his hunger satiated for now. In fact, the only thing that would make this better was a plum tart from his mother's kitchen. There had been a pair of plum trees that somehow managed to survive just on the edge of the warding circle back home. If he was careful, and under supervision, he was allowed to gather them when they were ripe and take them back to the house.

There were other fruit trees, and a few bask nut trees by the workshop, but they all lay outside the circle. And while they might have been fine, they also might have been corrupted by the menace from the south. Better to let them be. His father had told him once of a young man from the village who had gone and gathered all the nuts and fruit he could get to sell. He'd gathered a mighty amount, but hadn't realized that half were tainted with magic, and a Changer had snuck into a basket. He'd been attacked as he crossed the barrier at the village.

The Changer had died of course, but so had the man. And all the tainted fruit and nuts had rotted away before their eyes, tainting the remaining foodstuffs. You still heard of the occasional fool who dared others to gather off the trees. Usually, as some attempt to prove themselves, that they weren't *afraid* of magic. Though anyone who didn't avoid magic didn't tend to live that long.

"Now, before we retire till morning. Anchor Fean has given you permission to look inside your bench, and to take anything that interests you, as long as you carry it." Protector Binin smiled as she started clearing the table.

"Sartum guide us." Protector Wilk rolled his eyes and stopped off for his well-deserved and much-needed bath.

Layten had no idea what the Protector was talking about but realized the padded bench he'd been sitting on was more than a bench. It was storage. He carefully opened the top to see something that made his heart skip… books!

Chapter Eleven

Layten pulled several books out at once, too excited to read much but the titles. There wasn't a lot of them, only around ten. There were also three scrolls, each tied with red cord, and sealed with green wax. Layten left those in the storage; he was way too interested in the actual books. New books! He'd read every book they had at home more times than he could remember. He'd borrowed books when he could from traders and merchants, with the promise to return the next time they came. And of course, with the oath his father made to pay them if Layten lost anything.

But these were new ones. Books he'd never read. His hands were shaking as he opened each one to see what it was about. The first was a book on politics in Palnor, and the interactions between the Church of Sartum and the nobility. However, based on a note written at the bottom, the book was over a hundred years old, and so must be out of date.

The next was a set of two books, about the plants and animals native to the free lands, and an abbreviated list of magical creatures that one might get confused by. Highly useful for an Anchor, but for a scholar, less so. But it went into the maybe pile anyway. He knew what belonged in Lowter, but the rest of the North was spotty at best.

There were several journals of Anchors, just times, dates, and actions taken. He wasn't sure he should read those, but they, like the first book, were old. He placed the one with the best handwriting in the maybe pile as well. If he was going to read that, he didn't want to spend time wondering what word something was.

There was a book that was white, which was unusual. White leather wasn't cheap to make. He'd never seen a book covered in it before. It was small, and clean. Cleaner than the others, much less worn. He opened it to find that it was a half-handwritten history of the war of the breaking in the south. Whoever had started this had been meticulous in their details and clarity. He was disappointed to see it hadn't been finished though. There was also no date written on it anywhere, so he had no idea how old it might be.

I could finish it! Layten smiled at the thought. Yes, he could become a scholar and finish this, giving proper credit to whomever had done the first half. He could make this his journeyman project. All for the glory of Sartum of course. Yes, the more the idea came to him, the more he liked it. He placed the book in a new pile, the yes pile.

The three books remaining were also different. Two were pages and pages of drills and practices for Protectors. One was a book of geography, and relatively recent. He put that in the yes pile as well. If nothing else, since it had a few basic maps of the accursed south as well, it would help with the white book. The idea made him smile.

"Finding something you like?" Protector Binin was wiping down the counter, having put away everything while he'd been distracted by the treasure he'd been shown.

"Yes." Layten held up the two books he'd chosen. He also picked up one of the Protector's books. "Ever see this one before?"

Protector Binin walked over and took the book, nearly laughing as she did so. "The tactics of guardianship: a treatise. I haven't seen this in a very long time. And it's useless." Binin flipped through the pages. "No one uses these forms. There was a time when Protectors used overly complicated battle stances and were trained to use delicate and precise attacks and defenses. It looked pretty but was terribly silly and worthless in a fight." Layten hadn't heard any of that before and was curious. "What do you do now?"

"In training, Protectors receive training from a set of soldiers, mercenaries, and anyone who can show high skill with a blade, an axe, or a club. Spears and arrows too. Results matter, not how good you look doing it." Protector Binin shook her head and handed the book back to Layten. "That book got a lot of people killed, I'm sure."

"Do you actually have to fight all that often?" Layten hadn't really seen the Protectors fight anyone, or anything. "I mean, I could see something magical needing to be slain, but wouldn't the Anchor take care of that?"

"That is something you don't need to worry about." Protector Wilk walked into the room, now clean and dressed in what to Layten looked like the same leathers he always wore, just clean ones. "Put all that stuff away and go and get some rest. We have a long day tomorrow as well."

Layten felt his curiosity die. Wilk always shut everything down as soon as conversation got interesting. Still, he did have some new books to read, so that was useful. He placed the books back into storage minus the white book, and the geography one. Then in a moment of curiosity grabbed the book Binin had looked at, and just because, he took one of the scrolls. He'd not managed to look at those yet, and he had been told he could take anything as long as he carried it. Three books and one scroll weren't going to take up much room, or weight.

Layten grabbed his items and went back to his room for the night, yawning as he did so. He'd not been that tired before, but maybe as the excitement wore off, the day's events were wearing at him. He climbed into the small bed, happy with its softness. The light here was out, so he lit a small candle and flipped through the book on geography, trying to figure out which route they might take out of Giller.

His eyes closed soon after.

Anchor Fean cocked his head to one side, as if he were listening, then sat more upright. "Our traveling companion is asleep." He tapped the table a few times as both Protectors joined him at the table. "Are you sure it was him, Wilk?"

"Yes, Anchor. It was Nolmin. He'd only been dead a few weeks by the look of him. And the place had more resonance than I'd ever seen. It appears the whispers were more accurate than we'd thought." Protector Wilk shook his head.

"Was there any sign of his Protectors?" Binin looked down at the table. "I knew Bonti well. He was part of my training group."

"None. Whatever Nolmin had done, it doesn't appear his Protectors were part of it." Wilk crossed his arms. "The question now is what does this mean for our trip? First the Flitter and the Holant, and now this…" Wilk trailed off, his face turned towards the Anchor.

"My thoughts as well, Wilk. I am afraid that the situation has grown dire enough that I will have to commune with Sartum and seek a passage to drop off our companion and another to return to the Anchorhold." Fean shuddered for a moment. "I do not wish to even come close to knowing what this will cost me."

"If we could help you pay the price we would, you know that." Protector Binin spoke up. "I know why you took this trip, but the cost has been so high."

"I know. If I had known how badly things would go after we had left Lowter and Pol behind, I might not have come. But I did. And so, I must deal with the price." Anchor Fean held up his four-fingered hand. "I hope I do not have to pay a steeper price than that."

"As far as our companion, what are we going to do? You saw him react to that cabin." Wilk dropped his eyes. "You know what that might mean."

"You both agreed to never speak of this." Anchor Fean dropped his hand. His voice became sharp once more. "He is not to be dragged into this anymore than he already is. I will explain the passage. We will leave him at the gate, and then we will leave. He will go, live his life, and be happy. That is the end of it, do you BOTH understand?"

The Protectors exchanged glances, as the silence wore on for a moment before they both nodded. "What about his memories? Will you have to change anything again? That is dangerous, you know that," Binin asked, her voice low. "He's a good young man. He's suited to the life he's chosen. His face lit up when he saw the few books here. He took a few, not sure what exactly. Do you think the Anchors here will be upset?"

"Do you think any of them will argue with me?" Anchor Fean shook his head. "This is Giller. You know what Anchors end up here? Those who are already in trouble. Where did they go anyway, Wilk? You did a good job making them leave for the night."

"It wasn't that hard. I pointed out that you were coming, and it might be better if they were not here. The three of them and their Protectors found a reason to go patrol the hills to the south for a few days." Wilk smiled. "Based on how out of shape their Protectors were, might be a blessing for them."

Anchor Fean gave a sigh and pulled his hood free. "I hate wearing this hood. There's more going on. I was left information. A whole village in the Jolum mountains has vanished. The only things found were hundreds of holes, most the size of a large barrel, but all filled in. And one dead Gorbin."

Binin frowned. "Gorbins? I thought we pushed them out of that area years ago. It was a bloody affair. The things kept going underground to avoid the Anchors, so the Protectors had to storm tunnels to remove the things."

"Yes." Anchor Fean nodded and then made a frown. "The dead Gorbin had a letter on it, and a bag of copper. The note simply said, 'Payment for the food.'"

Wilk and Binin both looked sick at this news. "What is going to happen?" Wilk finally asked.

"I am not sure. The Anchorhold though can no longer wait. And… thank you, both of you." Anchor Fean pulled his hood up once more, hiding his face again. "You are our Anchor. It is our duty and honor." Protector Wilk thumped the table. "We are bound to you." Binin thumped the table as well, and the three shared a moment of silence.

Chapter Twelve

Layten awoke hungry. His stomach growled at him, still not recovered from missing lunch yesterday. The next body parts to make themselves well known were his back and thighs. Sore muscles yelled at him and were so stiff even sitting up in the bed was a challenge. It didn't help that the bed, while comfortable at first, had proved to be just too hard for his liking.

He tried to stretch, and managed to get a little bit more flexibility, but still felt as if he were walking around with knotted ropes instead of muscles in his back. He could smell food though, which helped him improve his mood. He moved carefully but managed to get ready faster than he'd feared. He got fully packed up and gingerly carried his pack back out to the common room. He'd not been told he had to do that, but it might make the Anchor and the Protectors think of him as more than a hanger-on. He felt a bit guilty at his earlier reluctance to travel with the Anchor, and with the time remaining he wanted to show he wasn't just some bumbling fool from Lowter.

He walked into the common room to find Binin frying some kind of fatty meat in a pan, and she already had a large stack of fried bread and another smaller pile of some kind of berries. "Ah, Layten. Good. And already packed. Even better." Protector Binin pulled what looked like a thin flat piece of pork laced with fat out of the pan, adding it to more of the same on a platter he'd not seen before. "Almost ready."

"Layten. There has been a change of plan." Anchor Fean strode into the room, his voice stern. "I am sorry, but the rest of us are needed back in the Anchorhold, today."

Layten tried to understand the words. "What? How could that even happen? Ture is weeks away, even at a fast gallop."

"Through Sartum, all things are possible." Anchor Fean waved to the table. "But do not fear. We will also get you to your destination today. Timik calls."

Layten was thrown off his mental plan. He'd be in Timik today? How? There was only one way of course, and the idea was a horrible one. Magic. He knew that for Anchors it was technically possible if the great God Sartum allowed them to use it. But didn't that just show how being around magic and working with it tainted a person? But to travel with magic over such a long distance... his skin felt ice cold and whatever appetite he had was now gone, replaced with a sour feeling in the bottom of his gut, and a metallic taste of bile in his mouth.

"Remember, magic used through the agency of Sartum is allowed, young Layten. We do not use it often, but if it is needed, and the God grants the boon, who are we to deny the will of Sartum?" Anchor Fean waved a still bandaged hand at the table. "We must eat, and then we travel."

Layten wasn't listening, he was staring at the hand. He was sure that the Anchor had all his fingers when they had first met. He would have noticed. But now? One was missing. The thought made Layten even sicker. The smell of the fat which had made his mouth water a few moments before now twisted him and made his head hurt.

"You aren't breaking any rules, Layten Grayread." Anchor Fean spoke again, for once his normally stern tone gone, making him sound almost kind, fatherly.

"I know." Layten wondered if the Anchor thought he was reacting this way because of the use of magic, or whatever it was going to be called. "I'll be… fine in a moment." Layten found himself wishing that the Anchor would put his hands away, so he wouldn't have to be reminded of the price he had paid. But why? What had happened that he didn't know about? As far as he knew, nothing interesting had happened the whole trip. Maybe when he was asleep? And they didn't want to worry him? Or maybe it had been missing before and he'd just not noticed. It wasn't like he spent a lot of time looking at someone's hands anyway.

The food was placed on the table, and Layten, despite not having much of an appetite now, did try to eat something. The berries at least were good and didn't make him feel slightly sick. He managed a few bites of the other items, enough at least that he felt that no one would ask him why he wasn't eating. "What do we do? What about the horses?" Layten asked, keeping his eyes off the Anchor.

"Your horse will be sent home; the others will come with us. They are… trained to deal with this in case it happens. Yours very much isn't, and that could cause some issues." Anchor Fean paused. "In fact, before we go, Wilk will give you something to drink. It will… make this easier for you."

"What? What is it?" Layten found himself curious despite the fear that gripped him. It was a very strange feeling, being both afraid enough that his hands were sweaty, and his stomach was unsteady, and wanting to know everything that was going to happen, and why.

"Not everyone can…process what is going to happen. We have no idea if you can. And there's not time to find out. So, the drink will make you…" Anchor Fean struggled to find the right word.

"It will make you drunk," Protector Binin added in. "Very drunk. Drunk enough that you won't care and won't even notice."

"Drunk?" Layten had only had a real drink twice. Once when his parents had signed a contract that had nearly doubled the money they made in a year, and once when he'd reached the right age, nineteen. Other than that, he hadn't drunk. He'd never been drunk. Despite himself he wondered what it would be like.

"Close enough. That's what I thought it felt like." Protector Binin shrugged. "Wilk?"

"It's kind of like that, kind of not." Wilk smiled. "But don't worry, it's very short-lived. We couldn't have you reporting to the House of Knowledge slurring your words and stumbling."

Layten hadn't even considered that. "Do I need to do anything?"

"No. Since you didn't eat all that much, it should work better anyway." Protector Wilk pulled a small pale violet vial out of a pocket. "This is what he was talking about. But not yet. Almost."

In short order they cleaned up and exited the building. The sun had risen, and the town of Giller was already in full movement. Two things struck Layten. One, it all looked far less impressive in the light of day. Sure, the place was far larger than home, but in the sun, the dark and formidable buildings showed their age and repairs. The other was just how much everyone avoided the area by the harbor. There must have been nearly 100 paces of empty space between the Harbor and the next buildings, and not a single person was walking through the open area, except of course for Layten and his companions.

Anchor Fean stood by his horse, as did the two Protectors. "Wilk, when it starts to form, please hand the vial to Layten. Layten, as soon as the vial is given to you, drink it. Drink it all."

Layten wondered what was in the liquid, exactly. He half wondered if he could drink it and keep the vial. Maybe he could find a way from any left on the glass to find out what it was. Would he learn things like that at the House of Knowledge? His growing excitement at finally reaching his goal made the abject terror at using magic, even a blessing from mighty Sartum, fade.

Anchor Fean grabbed his staff and raised it high, the blackness of it growing somehow larger. Layten's excitement faded into more terror as the air around him grew ice cold. A harsh empty void seemed to grow in his gut. A void reflected by the area in front of the Anchor that grew darker by the moment.

"Here, drink now." Protector Wilk thrust the vial into Layten's hands.

Layten uncorked the small vial and, with a slight hesitation, drank the vial in one gulp. He immediately wished he hadn't. The first thing he noticed was the consistency. Back home, the marsh reed beds would sometimes get this disease that made the water feel slick, almost like thin mud. This liquid had the same feeling. That was bad enough. The taste was worse. The first thing he tasted was metal. A horrible metal taste that coated his tongue. Then the fire came. A burning that didn't seem to end. Layten tried to gulp the air, and that just made it worse, for now the fire was mixed with ice.

He gasped, trying to not feel anything else yet still breathe. He'd use his nose, but nearly the same instant the fire had started, his nose had become so clogged as a reaction he couldn't take any air in through it. The fire mixed with the ice in a way that just brought pain, and absolutely no relief.

Thankfully it was short-lived, as the feelings faded and then… he fell into a state of complete unconsciousness.

Wilk watched as Layten reacted to the dastrin. Horrible stuff. At least the youth didn't choke; he had awareness enough to try and breathe through his mouth. But in a few moments the full effect hit him, and Layten stood there, completely gone. His body still moved, and would follow them, but he was, for all purposes, in a deep sleep.

"Lead on." Anchor Fean ordered Wilk to move forward. Wilk eyed the now totally black gap in the air in front of them. Big enough for them and the horses, it sucked in all the light, and the feeling of total cold emanated from its depths. He personally hated these things. Fean didn't use them much, and for that Wilk was very happy.

But an order was an order, and he was bound to Fean. He walked towards the blackness, keeping a tight rein on his horse in case the beast tried to run. Horses didn't like doing this either usually. Protectors' horses were trained to accept it, but that didn't mean they enjoyed it. That was the real reason they weren't bringing Layten's horse. The animal would have either hurt Layten in its terror to escape, or grown so scared it might have died, right there.

Stepping into the dark he could feel the cold gnaw at him. He knew from experience he just had to keep walking forward. Regardless of distance, he only had to take fifteen steps and he'd be at the other end, in this case right outside Timik, where the House of Knowledge was.

It was however a terrifying fifteen steps. You couldn't see anything; it was absolute black. It was horribly cold. The depths of winter had nothing on the cold here. If you entered one of these things on a hot summer day, you'd exit covered with ice and frost as all the sweat froze solid. But neither of these things were the worst part. The worst was the sounds.

The void was full of screams. Each person heard them differently. For Wilk, it was the screams of every person he'd ever had to kill, who had been an innocent. Mixed in was the screams and cries of his long-gone family. His mother, his sister, his long-dead wife, and even his son. All long gone, so long ago he had a hard time sometimes remembering their faces. But here, in this place, he heard them still. Screaming in pain, crying. Begging him to free them, to give them peace. There was no peace of course. They weren't real. It was this place. This… gap. The Anchors' staffs were similar in a way, and the warding circles. All related at least. That's what his training had told him, and he'd seen nothing to disabuse him of that belief. He was a Protector, so he didn't know the details, and Wilk had never wanted to know. He'd never met a Protector who did.

Wilk took his fifteenth step and the light blasted him, making his eyes snap shut. Relief flooded across him; the warmth of the sun tore the cold and sorrow from his skin. Even if it was colder here in Timik than Giller, it was far warmer than that place.

He was quickly followed by the Anchor, who was leading Layten as well, and finally Binin, who was pale and, based on the ice that had formed on her face, had been crying from the trip. He never asked either of them what they heard in that place. Some pains were too much to share.

Chapter Thirteen

The first thing Layten was aware of was the cold. Why was he so cold? In fact, he was colder than he'd ever been in his life. It never got that cold back home. Being near the water did that, or at least a trader had told him that once. His clothes were nearly stiff, with frost? The next thing to hit him was that the cold was fading quickly, and it was far brighter than it had been before. He'd been in Giller and had drunk whatever that vile stuff was that Protector Wilk had given him, and then, he was here. Here. Timik! He was in Timik! Or, he was supposed to be in Timik. His eyes weren't quite working right. He knew it was bright, and he was getting warmer, but other than that, he couldn't tell much.

"You'll be fine soon. Dastrin is potent stuff, but it doesn't last long, thankfully." Protector Wilk's voice came to him. "You can hear me, correct?"

"Yes." Layten forced the words out through chattering lips.

"The cold will fade as well. Sorry about that." Wilk almost sounded, friendly? Of all his traveling companions, the one he'd always gotten that go away feeling from was Wilk. And here the man was sounding almost concerned.

Layten blinked a few times, as shapes came into more focus. They were outside, on the side of a hill. And there, in the distance was… well it had to be Timik. But what a sight it was! Layten at once felt some shame at his overreaction to little Giller. Timik was, well... far more impressive in every way. A stone wall surrounded most of the city, taller than most trees that Layten had ever seen. A few gates, all massive even from here, could be seen.

Looming over the city in a few places were massive buildings, what they were he wasn't sure. One, the distance was too great, and two, his eyesight was still a little out of focus. The other thing he saw right away, was the people. A massive line of people was at each gate, and they just seemed to keep coming, both into the city and out of it.

"Yes, it's far more impressive than Giller. Timik is one of the five cities of the Houses. Timik, Gipol, Restu, Malin and, of course, Ture. So, this is worthy of being called a great city." Anchor Fean, still covered with his hood spoke. "Now, we will not be entering the city. But you will. You do have your papers, correct?"

Layten nodded, his thoughts still on the city in front of him. A real city. A real city that held the House of Knowledge. His goal. His dream. "Yes. I do." The words finally came, as he forced his eyes away from the sight in front of him. Focus on the here and now, right?

"Good." Anchor Fean waved to Binin who held out a small black scroll. A tiny thing, bound in silver cord. To Layten's eye, the paper was the strangest thing. It wasn't anything his father had made at least. "This will, hasten your entrance into the city. Once inside you will find someone who works for the House of Knowledge who will take you there.

"Thank you." Layten managed to say, the last of the chill had finally faded, and he was already warm now. "Thank you for getting me here as well. And…just thank you." He didn't know what to say about that drink or how they had gotten here, so he just left it at that.

Protector Binin laughed then, a pleasant sound. "Well, you are welcome, Layten Grayread. Truly. You weren't a bad traveling companion, all things accounted for." Protector Wilk just nodded and actually smiled. That left Anchor Fean, who kept his face towards the city. Finally, the Anchor talked. "It has been a pleasure, Layten. Write home. I'm sure your parents will want to know you made it here fine. I wish you a long and happy life in the House of Knowledge."

Layten nodded. The Anchor was still a mystery to him. Why did he never show his face? He'd had this strange feeling since that first night that there was something he was missing, something just out of reach. But it always faded soon after the thought came. "Thank you, Anchor. I will," he finally said.

"Here's your pack, now go!" Binin smiled as she thrust the pack into Layten's chest, and he took his first step towards the city below and his new life. He walked a short distance before turning back to see them already gone. If they had just walked out of sight or used that… thing to leave he didn't know. But it was better he not know, right?

He pushed any thoughts of magic, or using magic, away from him, it wasn't something he needed to dwell on. He walked at a steady pace, and while outwardly he appeared calm, he was anything but. He was here! In Timik. His long sought-after goal, right here in front of him. Layten soon found himself in the stream of people moving toward the closest gate. In front of him was a man riding in a small cart, full of huge earthen jars. Layten could hear things sloshing around in them, but what it was he didn't know.

Behind him was a pair of women, each carrying what must have been a very heavy basket of bright red and orange cloth on their heads. He'd never seen anyone do that before, and he wondered if their neck hurt all the time. Still the line went smoothly, even if it was a little dusty, smelly, and loud. That was the first thing Layten had noticed that bothered him. It was so loud here. A constant rumble seemed to fill the air, interspersed with sharp coughs, laughs, sneezes, yells of anger or annoyance. Layten clenched his jaw and the assault on his hearing. He hadn't expected this to be the one thing that bothered him the most.

Finally, he was at the gate. The man with the cart had made it through, but only after showing the rather bored looking man in a grey and green tabard what was in the jars. Layten half wondered what was in the things himself, if only to pass the time while he waited.

"Name and purpose of visit?" The man's eyes didn't even leave the marking slate in front of him.

"Layten Grayread. New member of the House of Knowledge." Layten didn't think this would be too hard, why had the Anchor given him that token scroll?

"Hmmm." The man finally looked up and gave Layten a look over. "Where from?"

"Lowter." Layten didn't hesitate to say the word, though he wanted to. Lowter was just that, low. Poor, small, and far too close to the southern border to be… acceptable.

A smirk creased the man's face. "Lowter? The House of Knowledge doesn't take people from Lowter. Go away."

"My father is the papermaker for the House. He helped." Layten held up the papers he had. "They are awaiting me."

"And my father is the head of the House of Blood in Restu. Go away." The man waved the two women forward, ignoring Layten's grimace.

"I'm not done." Layten pulled out the small black scroll the Anchor had given him. The effect was somewhat satisfying. The man who had just dismissed him out of hand went wide-eyed, just for a moment, before stopping the two women.

"Ah, very sorry." The man marked down Layten's name, but only after asking him how it was all spelled three times, as he kept getting flustered.

"Go on." The official waved Layten through without another word and turned his entire attention to the two women who had been waiting.

Layten found this all very strange, but again, did it matter right now? The Anchor had been very vague about finding someone to take him to the House of Knowledge. He'd never really thought that far ahead, a fact that embarrassed him. He hadn't thought it through. Something he always did. Layten was careful, and planned every step, normally.

He stood on the edge of a large square, with merchants waving things around, and enough people walking around and everywhere that Layten couldn't even follow anyone, they all got lost in the mess. Finally, he spotted a small banner with the insignia of the House of Knowledge on it. A pair of scrolls over a large tome that bore the image of a city and a bloody hammer, the sigil of Sartum.

Layten pushed forward, drawing a few curses and a shove as he crossed the courtyard. He was sure at least once someone tried to rifle through a pocket or two, but everything he owned of value was in his pack, which he was clutching to his chest. If a would-be pickpocket struck, at best they would get an interesting piece of wood, badly worked to resemble an animal, though what animal was an open question.

He stepped inside the small room, and felt his second real shock, as sitting behind a counter, was a Gorom. An actual living Gorom. Gorom were the first non-humans to see the truth of Sartum and had switched their allegiance from whatever god they had used to follow to Sartum. Gorom however were rare. Very rare. Layten had never been able to discern why.

"Hello?" Layten didn't want to disturb the Gorom if the thing was asleep. It sure appeared that way. Its cowl, drawn tight, hid its face, the lighting was very dim, and no sound seemed to penetrate from outside.

"What?" A voice came that rumbled, and almost echoed in the space. The Gorom, which had been leaning back in repose, sat up and pushed the cowl of its hood up, exposing its chin.

"My name is Layten Grayread. I'm here to start my training at the House of Knowledge. But I have no idea how to get there." Layten couldn't help but stare as when the Gorom spoke, skin as white as any cloth or paper he'd ever made appeared in the parts of the face he could make out.

"Hrmmpph." The Gorom pushed his cowl down. "Show me the letters."

Layten did stare then. The Gorom was bald, and as white as snow, as blued wood pulp, as… anything white. What hair he did have was a wispy beard, and even wispier eyebrows. There was a single glowing thing right at his neckline that vanished as the Gorom noticed him staring.

"What? Never seen a Gorom before?" The Gorom nearly sneered as he spoke.

"No. I haven't." Layten answered truthfully. "There are none where I live. Or lived I suppose."

"Huh?" The Gorom held out his hand. "Letters?"

Layten pulled the small grouping of letters together. Each one standing for years of dreaming and work. Even if his father's word had helped, Layten had still done the work. He'd once spent two full weeks at night carefully learning the high script. Practicing it until his hand was nothing more than a claw the next day.

The Gorom flipped through the letters, pausing and muttering a few times before handing the stack back to Layten. "Lowter? No wonder you've never seen a Gorom. Lowter is mud, forests, and bugs. And that's about it."

Layten wanted to argue, but the truth was, the Gorom was right. "How do I get there?" He asked again, not wanting to be drawn off into discussing the trade goods of Lowter, such as they are.

"Well, I'm heading there myself. So, you can follow me." The Gorom slid off the short stool he'd been sitting on. "Keep up."

Chapter Fourteen

Layten found himself scrambling to keep up with the pace the Gorom was making, as he seemed to be running or floating even through the crowds. Layten had apologized nearly a dozen times for running into people before the Gorom stopped and stared at him. "What are you doing? Why are you so slow?" The Gorom had put his hood back up, but the pale skin was still evident.

"You are moving so fast." Layten tried to say, before the Gorom pulled him over to the side, and out of the flow of traffic.

"Let me guess, you are from what, Lowter? It's always places like Lowter. Everything is small and doesn't have a name worth remembering." The Gorom rubbed his chin in thought. "You don't need to apologize to anyone. This is Timik. They don't care. They don't think about you. They don't want to know you. They don't want to talk to you."

Layten was surprised by his reaction to the disparaging of Lowter. He was annoyed. Lowter wasn't some great place, but it was home. "Lowter isn't fancy or big, but…." He trailed off shrugging. He realized he didn't like this Gorom much. The man seemed to treat everything with irritation and disgust.

"Just keep up." The Gorom headed back into the flow of people, and Layten, this time kept up better. He still wanted to stop and apologize, but he realized no one else was either. They just pushed past anyone moving slower and didn't even blink. He once saw someone looking at a stall get nearly pushed into the table, and no one even blinked. So, this is Timik??

Finally, the Gorom turned off onto a smaller street with fewer vendors. Smaller did not mean dirtier though. The street was in all actuality far grander. And held shops that seemed to be more catered to the House of Knowledge. Ink makers, bookbinders, and of course the frequent loud and noisy inns were passed. One claimed to be a paper and scroll seller, which of course drew his attention, but the Gorom didn't stop so there was no time to look.

Finally, the Gorom turned down another street and stopped in front of a grand door. Engravings of books and scrolls, pen motifs, marking rods mostly, older style work. This had to be the place. Layten looked up and the building the door was attached to did not seem all that large, but he couldn't see how deep it was, maybe it was bigger than it appeared from right here.

"Well, here you go. Now we wait for a guard to appear. You hand him your letters, and then we go in." The Gorom crossed his arms and waited in silence.

Layten joined him but felt his nerves growing. Now that he was here, he didn't know what to say. What to do.

"Are there a lot of Gorom here at the House of Knowledge?" he finally asked, trying to fill the silence.

"No. there are not a lot of Gorom anywhere. I am the only one in all Timik." The Gorom scowled at the door. "Fools are being lazy again."

"No other Gorom here at all?" Layten was slightly surprised by this information. "But Gorom are special! They were the first race not of Sartum's creation to see and understand the truth of the joined God!"

The Gorom turned to him, his expression one of surprise and, if anything, disgust. "You are going to be a scholar? Ha! Learn the truth. My people are almost gone, faded from this world. And you humans, all you ever see is a Gorom. Do you know you never even asked my name?"

Layten opened his mouth to protest but closed it again. The Gorom was right. And he'd been thinking of the man as a thing, an 'it.' "Well, you are right. I am sorry. What is your name?"

The Gorom's frown slid a little off his face. "Maybe there is hope for you. My name is Waiter-in-the-Halls. But for the most part, humans, being, well, humans, just call me Halls."

"Halls?" Layten didn't understand the name. He had a lot to learn about Gorom it appeared.

"Waiter-in-the-Halls. But it's fine. Humans have never understood our ways." Halls tapped at the door. "Wake up, Eimin. You've left me out here too long." Halls yelled the words.

The door opened a crack. "Halls! Were you waiting out there? But then again, that's your job isn't it, to wait?" A man clad in a brown and blue robe opened the door, stepping out.

"Shut it, Eimin. Have a new apprentice here. He's got his letters." Halls motioned for Layten to step up.

"Oh?" Eimin reached out a hand towards Layten, his eyes wide.

Layten wasn't sure he liked this man. He had the hands of a writer though. He had several ink stains on his right hand, and most of them were old. Even the hem of his right sleeve showed ink on it, and it all looked worn. But that wasn't what made him uneasy. It was his eyes.

His eyes were wide, but Layten could see it didn't translate to his eyebrows. He was faking surprise. The man just felt, fake. But that didn't really matter right now, he had to give him his letters, right? The fluttering in his stomach didn't help, but Layten handed over his letters of admittance. Letters he'd been guarding since the day a trader had brought them.

"Oh…. Layten Grayread." Eimin rolled his eyes. "Lowter. We don't take people from Lowter. These must be fake." Eimin threw the letters onto the cobblestones. "Really, Halls? Bringing a fake apprentice here just to annoy me?"

"He's not fake." Halls grumbled. "Think, Eimin, if all that drink you partake of hasn't addled your wits."

"He's a Lowter! We don't take them. At best they can get into the House of Blood, or maybe Song, if that hideous accent doesn't do them in." Eimin raised a foot to grind the letters into the ground.

"No!" Layten rushed forward, pushing Eimin over and grabbing his precious letters before this man could do anything to him.

"EIMIN!" A thundering voice came from behind this Eimin person. "What in Sartum's name are you doing?"

"Just sending away a bad joke by Halls," Eimin yelled back, pushing Layten away. "GO away, Layten Grayread."

"Grayread?" The loud voice came again. "Layten Grayread?" A thick figure of a man came from the shadows. "I know the Grayread name."

"My father is Unil Grayread. Grayread paper is used here." Layten kept his eyes off Eimin now. It was obvious who had the actual power here, and it wasn't that fool.

"Yes! Yes! You wrote a very good example of your
work for your application. Very good indeed." The
thick man turned to Eimin, who was now truly
surprised, though the venom laced with that look wasn't
anything Layten liked.

"Your foolish attitude isn't helping, Eimin. The
Grayreads make the best paper in the north. And we use
a lot of it. This is the son of Unil Grayread, and he HAS
been accepted into the House. Did you actually
examine the letters before you acted like an idiot?" The
thick man turned his attention back to Layten.

"Very sorry. Eimin here is a… long-term student. We
sometimes let him help out with things like the door
when it's not busy. You are early, we weren't expecting
the new apprentices for a week at least. My name is
Triwek. Triwek Dolomin. I am the Keeper of the
second gate." Triwek offered Layten his hand, along
with a smile.

This Layten took, with a smile. He liked this man, if
only because he put Eimin in his place somewhat.

"Thank you, Scholar Dolomin. And thank you, Waiter-
in-the-Halls." Layten gave the Gorom a slight bow,
which managed to draw a small smile from the acerbic
Gorom.

"I apologize for being so early." Layten started to
explain about the Anchor but stopped suddenly. He
wasn't sure what he could say. "I... came with someone
who left earlier than I had expected."

"Oh, no problem. Come in, come in." Scholar Dolomin
waved him through the gated doors and into the House
of Knowledge.

Layten followed his lead, stepping into a hall that seemed far too large for the building. The air smelled clean, if not for the ever-present scent of paper, and ink. It reminded him of home. The door closed behind him with a click, as Eimin closed it and stalked off, his movements quick and stiff, as if to say he didn't care one bit about Layten and what had just happened.

"What about Waiter-in-the-Halls?" Layten turned around but there was no sign of the Gorom. "He said he was coming here for something as well."

"Halls? He was, to bring you. That's his job. He's a grumpy one. But then all Gorom are. Or were. Outside of Halls I've only ever met two other Gorom. Not many of them left." Scholar Dolomin beckoned Layten to follow him deeper into the House of Knowledge. Layten did so, his eyes darting from door to door trying to read the small plaques that labeled each one. Ink storage? Scroll storage? Lesser library one? A highly tarnished plaque couldn't be read at all, at least not at the pace the Scholar was setting. For a man his size, he had a fast gait, though not nearly as fast as the Gorom had been.

"Come along, come along." Triwek led Layten through half a dozen twists and turns before finally he stopped at a large wooden door with a plaque that just read 'One.' "Ah! First-year apprentice lodging. I am afraid you are actually the first to arrive, so it will be rather quiet for a few days. The whole House will be quiet, until the new term starts."

"Quiet is fine." Layten was more than happy with quiet. "Is there a room assigned to me?"

"Well, let me check here…" Scholar Dolomin opened the door to show a small table with a large book on it. He flipped through the book, passing what looked like years in rows and tables of names and locations. After a good amount of flipping, he stopped at a half-full page. "Here we are. Oh ho! You have a triple. Those are nice rooms, larger by far than most. The two other first years aren't here yet, but you can move in. Give you a few days to get your bearings anyway, the House of Knowledge was built by Sartum himself, you know. Like all the other Houses. As a result, it's…special. It is bigger on the inside, by Sartum's blessing. You are in room four."

Layten felt his skin crawl at that. More magic. The idea would have made him vomit, if he had let it. "Oh." Was all he managed to say, working to keep the distaste out of his mouth, and voice.

"Get organized. There's a closet at the end of the hall here that has your robes and first-year supplies. Take three robes, no more mind you, and no less. And ONE kit. Had a first-year take eight once and tried to sell them out on the street. Fool got himself expelled in the first week." Scholar Dolomin shook his head. "Not that you would do such a thing."

"No, I wouldn't." Layten was itching to explore now, and he pushed his distaste of the idea of magic away. Now was not the time.

"Good. Good. So, get your items, and get settled. I will come and get you when it's time to eat. Finding your way can be tricky at first. It's better however to stay in this wing and not wander. Some parts of the House are not for everyone, and… it's just better you stay in this wing. There is a small student study at the end of the hall as well, it only has a thousand books in it, but that should stave off too much boredom." Scholar Dolomin waved goodbye, leaving Layten the shocked one as the door closed, leaving Layten alone.

Chapter Fifteen

A thousand books? Layten couldn't even conceive of that many books in one place. And that was a small library? He fought the urge to run to this small library and explore it right away, deciding that he'd do that after he'd done everything else. It wasn't like there was a rush, he was the only one here, right? The hall was spacious if plain. Unlike the other parts of the House he'd seen, this hall had little decoration. It all appeared worn as well, which at first disappointed him.

But if this had been the apprentice quarters for a long time, that wasn't overly surprising. The idea of generations of scholars walking these halls, rubbing the stone smooth in places, their hands removing the corners of square door frames over years until they were now mostly round was one he rather liked the more he thought about it. Permanence. Yes, that was it, permanence.

He found his room and opened it to find a rather large room with a single door leading off to what must be the bathing chambers. There were three large beds, and three desks, and three bookshelves arranged carefully so anyone could tell which belonged to whom. Layten considered his options and took the bed that was more tucked into the corner, away from the main door, and on the opposite wall of the bathing area.

The bed was soft and, much to his surprise, was stuffed with actual down, not moss. He at once pictured his mother, Reina, pondering how to keep all that down clean and vermin free. Then he realized it. He'd not seen a single spider, or any kind of bug since he'd entered here. And… no smoke. He turned to the lamp that was lit and supplying light to his room. That wasn't fire, it was something else.

The feeling of darkness, of a cold and empty void filled him again. More magic. Layten didn't like it at all. All this use of that dark power underlying everything. Even if it was a power given by Sartum. He knew the words of High Prophet Jinir. *Magic is a gift from the God. Only Sartum has the knowledge and will to know what a good use of the power is. Anything else is an abomination. Magic was not meant for mortals to use directly.*

That didn't help his empty feeling, and he longed for a simple candle, not this strange lamp. He knew a candle was impossible of course, while no one had said it directly to him, at least not yet, it made sense that fire was a decidedly dangerous idea in a place like this. Layten, with some effort, turned his attention away from the idea of magic and concentrated on getting things organized instead. He unpacked what few things he had with him. Some clothes, the barely, if at all, used journal he'd brought. The books and single scroll from the Anchorhold in Giller. He had no idea what the scroll was. Maybe he'd investigate that later if he got bored.

The white journal and the book of Protector exercises and tactics was put on the bookshelf, looking rather silly sitting there alone. He knew it wouldn't be alone for long, a fact he was looking forward to. The idea of just learning things banished the lingering uneasiness about the magic being used here and brought a bit of a bounce to his step. He exited the room, making his way to the end of the hall, finding the room with the robes and, to his somewhat delight, what must be the kits the Scholar had spoken about.

The robes were serviceable, and felt comfortable to the touch, though Layten knew he would feel slightly strange wearing robes. He'd never worn anything like that before. It was, however, what he was supposed to wear, so that was that. He found three that fit fine, and turned his attention to the kits, which were far more interesting to him.

Each consisted of a large rucksack type of bag, that was stuffed with ink, blue, black, red, and a rather different silver-looking ink. Multiple pens, both the old-fashioned marking rods, and the newer style. A small selection of paints, with a few tiny brushes. And of course, paper. Some was loose, but most were in the form of four blank books. Each one plain leather over wood covers, and everyone embossed with a number, one through four.

It was the quality of the paper that struck him the most. It wasn't Grayread paper. That was obvious. The felting was wrong, and it was too white. Wherever this had come from, they had rubbed far too much clay into it. He took a loose piece and tried to tear a small corner off. It gave way quickly, releasing a wave of dust as it did so. Not good binders either. Bulk work. That did disappoint him some, but it made sense to save good materials for students who knew what they were doing. At the bottom of the rucksack was a set of measuring rods, and an odd thing. It was three metal rings, each wound through each other, locking them into place. It was heavy as well, solid. Layten's close inspection showed no seams, no dents, nothing. It was also cold. Very cold. Colder than the room was by a significant margin. Layten spent a few moments trying to shift a ring free, wondering if it was a puzzle or a game.

After a few minutes he shrugged and put it back in the rucksack. The downside to being the only person here was he couldn't talk to anyone. He liked the quiet, but asking questions made him happy. He liked to KNOW things. Asking questions was part of that.

He carried the robes and kit back to his room and decided on his next steps. At some point Scholar Dolomin was supposed to come get him to eat. He'd not had anything to eat since the Giller Anchorhold, and he was hungry. But he didn't know when that would be exactly. He eyed his journal and some of the loose paper from the rucksack. He needed to write a letter home as well, he'd promised Anchor Fean and his parents that he would. His anger towards them had cooled considerably now that he'd seen a few magical things already, and he knew how wrong it made him feel. It was probably better that they had made him forget, as much as he didn't like it. Now he was more upset that no one had asked him first.

But was he going to hold a grudge over it? No. He was at the House of Knowledge. If things went well, he'd not go home for years, if ever. He didn't want his anger to be the last thing his parents heard from him. But... he had no idea how to get it to them. He'd ask the Scholar tonight, then write it. That left the library. Layten started to seek it out but stopped. He was in the House of Knowledge. He was going to one of the libraries and was waiting for a Scholar to come get him for dinner. He should be dressed for the part, right?

He cleaned up first of course. He washed his face and hands and wet his hair down enough that using a small comb he could at least make a good show of trying to tame the unruly mess. Finally, he put on the robes, feeling the softness, and the odd weight of the garment. He hoped he was wearing it correctly, some of the ties and buttons were confusing. Still, he felt like it was right when he was done. If it wasn't, someone would tell him, of that he was sure.

He examined himself in the small, polished stone mirror they provided and was pleasantly surprised to see a clean, well-groomed, robed young scholar in the reflection. That was what he was supposed to be, and the feeling brought a surge of pride.

He exited his room and went back to the end of the hall. The door was oddly hidden by the paneling of the walls, and the plaque marking its location was tarnished to the point that you had to be right up on that location to see it. The door, as hidden as it was, still slid open with a small touch. A new wonder filled Layten's eyes. Books. Hundreds of books. All laid out and organized. More books than Layten had ever seen in one place. Layten found himself walking through the room, his fingers running along the spines as he read the titles. *On the habits of the grayling ground squirrel. The clothes of the Lesser Imperium period. Cooking on horseback: a culinary tour of the borderlands.* Layten found himself wondering why these books existed at all. Silly titles, for books that should have never been written. Where was the meat?

"Ah! I see you've found this little study. And you are dressed correctly for dinner! Good, good." Scholar Dolomin opened the door to the room Layten was in. Layten could tell his decision to put on the robe was the correct one, if just based on the smile Scholar Dolomin was sporting. "Come, it's time to eat. I'll introduce you to a few others here right now. By this time, in a few days, these halls will be overflowing with students. But for now, it's very much the bare minimum."

Layten took one more look at the study, wishing he felt better about the books. He should be overjoyed, but they all seemed, weak in some way. Useless? No, just... frivolous. Making a book was a time-consuming process. It took time and talent. Why use such artisanship for such esoteric and mostly unneeded writing? The Scholar was still waiting for him though, so his thoughts would have to wait.

"Come on. I'm sure the food will be getting cold if we don't get to moving." Scholar Dolomin led the way out into the House of Knowledge.

Chapter Sixteen

Layten followed the Scholar, still finding himself conflicted about the House of Knowledge as a whole. He was happy to be here, so much so at moments he felt like he would laugh loudly at the sheer joy of it. But the constant use of magic, and the fact the whole place was saturated with that wrongness, gave him the shivers. They passed several large doors that were marked with the word 'Gate' and a number. He didn't know what those were. Hadn't the Scholar introduced himself with something gate in a title?

Layten wished he'd paid more attention to that. He was going to be a scholar; he was supposed to always pay attention. But he'd been so annoyed by the fool at the door earlier, he'd not been as focused on everything else. "Excuse me, Scholar Dolomin? What does that Gate thing mean? You said something about a second gate? And I see doors labeled 'Gate' and a number?"

The Scholar paused for a moment. "Well, that's a fair question. We go over all that during the first training when all the apprentices are here. But I'll say this much. The House of Knowledge holds things that are dangerous. Those things are protected by gates. I am the head scholar of the second gate. It goes up to the fourth gate. As an apprentice, you don't get access to a gated area at all. Sort of a gate zero. Those areas we passed are for those who have been accepted into that gate."

"Marked? Marked how? And what could be dangerous here?" Layten pushed for more information, but as soon as the words left his mouth, he rather regretted it. "Sorry, Scholar Dolomin."

To his relief the Scholar laughed. "No apologies needed. You're a scholar. We ask questions. But let's get to the dining hall and then I'll say what I can. Besides, this isn't going to support itself!" The Scholar slapped his midsection, making a loud smack. He turned to Layten with a grin and waved his hand to follow.

Layten's shoulders relaxed some at this display. He had hoped he'd not overstepped his bounds, and it didn't appear he had. He would hopefully get more answers, and food at the same time, a good thing all around. Layten instead turned his mind to remembering his way back to the apprentice halls. It wasn't THAT far of a walk, it just all looked very similar. In short order though, they stopped at a door the size of a full wagon. "Here we are!" Scholar Dolomin pushed at the doors that, much to Layten's surprise, opened smoothly and without a noise.

A cavernous room greeted them, a room full of tables, but none had chairs at them except for a small one nearest to the far wall. There were already three people sitting there eating. "Good. You will meet some of the others here now. Trust me when I say this place will be much louder and more alive."

Layten followed him as he weaved around to the table. He found himself less interested however when he realized that one of the people there was the fool at the door from before, Einim. The other two he didn't know, however. One was a kindly looking woman, almost like a Grandmother. Her hair was white and fine but pulled up tight, so it didn't fall free. To Layten it almost looked like marsh fungus. He did not give voice to this fact. The other was a shock. It wasn't a human. Or a Gorom. It was a Trinil. What was a Trinil doing here? If the woman looked kind and sweet, this Trinil appeared to be almost the opposite. His face was set in a frown, and the lines around it showed this was a common occurrence.

Layten was happy to see that everything he'd read about Trinil, which wasn't much truthfully, had been correct. The thing was tall, thin, and looked rather stretched. Its hair was long and glossy and had an odd greenish silver sheen to it. All three of them were eating some kind of soup, or broth. There was a large communal pot in the middle of the table with plates of bread, fruit, cheese, and even one small plate of tarts or pies. The sight brought back some of his hunger, as the last few days of decidedly less than three meals a day had started to catch up with him.

"Ah, Triwek!" The woman spoke first, looking up from her bowl. "And who is this with you dressed in apprentice robes?"

"Dine, this is Apprentice Layten Grayread. He arrived earlier today. He wasn't due till next week, but those he traveled with left earlier. Layten, this is Dine Nimer. She is the Scholar of the first Gate, and the keeper of supplies for all apprentices and journeymen." Scholar Dolomin then turned his attention to the Trinil. "And this is Master Retuin. He is here often, but he is not one of us. He's…"

"I am the one who makes the inks." The Trinil spoke, his voice strange. Layten could only describe it as slightly hollow, like speaking through a hollow log. "All the inks. And your name... Grayread?"

Layten nodded. As soon as this Master Retuin had said what he did he knew this question was coming. "Yes, my father is Unil Grayread, and my mother is Reina."

"Ah." Master Retuin placed his spoon down and looked at Layten with a much more appraising look. "Your parents do very good work. The quality of their paper is perfect for some of my more…interesting projects." Layten had no idea what this Trinil meant, but nodded anyway, if just for the fact that he'd complimented his parents' work. And in a way his own work since he'd been part of his family's business for several years before he left. He took a seat as far from Eimin as possible and began to fill a bowl and gather some of the other items.

He knew it was obvious that he was keeping his distance and not talking to Eimin, but he wasn't sure he really cared. At the time he'd been frustrated and surprised. Now he was just mad. Thankfully Eimin seemed to be happy to ignore his presence as well, a fact Layten was happy to continue.

"So, Apprentice Grayread, what do you think of the House of Knowledge so far? Did you find your kit? What did you think of it?" Scholar Nimer arched an eyebrow as if she was examining a potential flaw in a book.

"It's something. I've never seen anything like it." Layten was truthful and wondered just how truthful he should be. "The kit was interesting. Thank you. I don't understand the purpose of the three-ring thing, but I'm sure it will become clear, sometime." He left off his poor impressions of the paper, though.

"Oh really? All of it was good?" Scholar Nimer put her spoon down and gently folded her hands into her lap. Layten realized he'd made a mistake. She was looking for a comment on the one thing he'd let pass. "Well, the paper was substandard. Too much of a clay wash, poor binders. But since it's for apprentices, I thought it was just cheap stock to use."

Layten wondered now if he'd gone too far, as the mouth of Scholar Nimer drew into a tight circle, one that brought deep wrinkles to what had been a happy face. Then, just as quickly she laughed, transforming that sour look into one of humor and joy. "Well said! Yes, I was just curious what you thought."

Eimin mumbled something, but it couldn't be heard since his face was nearly low enough to be in his bowl. Layten was happy that everyone ignored whatever the mumble had been. For his part Layten just wanted to eat now. And eat he did. The soup was good if basic. A barley soup, with some herb he'd never tasted before, almost sour, but it cut some of the richness from the cream. The bread was good, though unfamiliar, and slightly sweet. Dark too, almost as dark as black sugar.

But everything was good, and Layten soon finished off his bowl and plate. No one objected to him getting more though, and he tucked into a second bowl. Eimin soon left, not even looking at Layten as he did so. He did however give a bow to the Scholars, but also ignored this Master Retuin. The Trinil for his part ate mostly fruit and some of the bread. He did however spend a large amount of time looking at Layten, a fact that made him somewhat uncomfortable.

"Master Retuin, I did not expect to see a Trinil here." Layten finally got sick of the visual inspection and put down his own spoon and pushed the remnants of his food away. "Or anywhere in the free lands."

The Trinil gave a small smile and nodded his head. "Reasonable. I might be one of maybe a dozen of my kin who are here in these lands. There are not many. But considering I do follow Sartum, and my skills are useful. Here I am."

This was a surprise to Layten, he'd not heard of any Trinil following the true god of Alos, Sartum. "You follow Sartum?" his voice rose with each word. "I had no idea."

"There aren't many who do." Master Retuin took a last bite of some bright green fruit that Layten had passed up, since he had no idea what it was. "Not many at all." He added with a smile.

"Ah." Layten got the meaning. Only a dozen and they all lived in the North. Noted and hopefully would be remembered. "Scholar Dolomin, thank you again for helping me today."

"Nonsense. Even if you hadn't been a Grayread, I would have. Eimin was… out of line." The pause given in his words was obvious.

Layten wondered if that kind of behavior was normal for the man and couldn't begin to understand why they'd let him ever be at the door. Though he did remember the Scholar saying something about letting him do it because they hadn't expected anyone. "Still, I appreciate it."

"So, do you have questions about anything you've seen so far?" Scholar Nimer added. "I ask as the Keeper of the first gate."

"Well…" Layten did wonder about the books. "The books in the apprentice area, why are they so…." Layten struggled to come up with the right word for them.

"Useless?" Scholar Nimer smiled as she spoke. "Well, what you see there are the results of something all apprentices must do. Make a book. And the subject matter must be original. So, after several hundred years…."

"The things to write about get worse and worse," Layten added. It made sense, though he didn't see the point, not fully.

"I wouldn't say worse. I would say more, esoteric. All knowledge is worth something, Apprentice Grayread. It may not be useful to you, or me, or anything else here. But it still has value." Scholar Nimer stood, brushing a loose crumb from her robes, which mirrored the robes Scholar Dolomin wore.

"My apologies. You are right." Layten did not want to get into an argument with a Scholar.

"Don't apologize. Just learn from it. Now, in a short few days most of the staff will be back, teachers, support staff, everything. Then in a few days after that, the students will return. This may be the last time I actually speak to you one-on-one, Apprentice. So, welcome. I look forward to seeing you grow here in knowledge and truth." Scholar Nimer nodded her head at Layten as she exited via a small door that Layten hadn't noticed before.

"She likes you. Normally she just runs roughshod over Apprentices." Master Retuin sniffed and stood himself. "Good evening to you all," he stated but kept his eyes on Layten before leaving in the same direction that Scholar Nimer had.

"Well then." Scholar Dolomin stood as well. "Welcome to the House of Knowledge."

"Thank you." Layten stood as well, looking down at the dishes. "There must be staff to clean this?"

"There will be." Scholar Dolomin gave Layten a half apologetic look. "But you are an apprentice, so have fun cleaning this up. That door there leads to the scullery. I trust you can find your way back to your room?"

Layten didn't know what to say, so he just nodded, and watched the Scholar leave the room. "Dishes… great." Then he rolled up his sleeves and got to work.

Chapter Seventeen

Layten sighed, throwing down the towel after having spent the last two bells scrubbing, rinsing, and drying more dishes than he'd ever seen in his short life. The table dishes weren't bad, but the scullery had been full. Whoever had made that meal had used enough dishes to feed a small army, he was sure of it. But it was done. He hoped it wouldn't be a normal requirement for him. Still, it had allowed him some time to think. The Trinil being here still made him wonder some. He'd never heard of one of them ever being a follower of Sartum, though Master Retuin had said there were a rare dozen or so who did. He was happy that more were seeing the truth of the Unsundered God, though. Did these Trinil still have the purported ability to always know if someone was lying to them? That was a skill he wished he had. Invaluable for a scholar, to always know the truth.

He dried his hands again, frowning at the slightly pale and wrinkled skin. They'd get back to normal fast enough, but he had wanted to make some notes and questions, and writing like this always made him feel like he didn't have a good grip on anything. Leaving the scullery, he tried to make sure he knew which way to go, but in short order he realized he'd take a wrong turn somewhere. He was surrounded by doors and plaques he didn't understand.

"I apologize for earlier, Apprentice Grayread." A voice came from around a corner, a voice that Layten already didn't like much, Eimin. Still, it was an apology.

"Apology accepted." Layten was polite. He really didn't want to get into a fight here with someone who'd been around for a long time. Even if he didn't like the man.

"We were never formally introduced. Senior Journeyman Eimin Galatine. As close to full Scholar as one can get, I suppose, without being a full Scholar." Eimin flashed a smile.

Layten wanted to ask why he fell short, just to poke the man for his rudeness at the gate. But he let it pass. "Good to know. Journeyman Galatine, I seem to be lost. How do I get back to the apprentice wing from here?"

"Senior Journeyman." Eimin's voice dropped a notch. "Do not forget that Apprentice."

Layten's already low opinion of the man dropped further. "Senior Journeyman Galatine, my apologies."

"What did you say? Oh yes, apology accepted." Eimin smiled again.

Layten knew the man must think himself so clever to throw that out. To Layten he just looked petty. "Senior Journeyman Galatine, I appear to be lost."

"A common enough occurrence for those, who like you, come from… less educated homelands. If you had grown up in a proper city, this would be easy. But don't worry, I shall help you find your way." Eimin stood up straight and waved a hand in a slightly imperious way. Layten for his part tried very hard not to laugh. Eimin Galatine was not a tall man. In fact, he was a good half a hand shorter than Layten was. So, the effect of his actions just made him look like a puffed-up fool, not anything superior. "I would be thankful for your help," he managed to say without breaking into the laughter he was holding onto.

"It is simple. Down this hall, turn right. Then four doors down, open the door on the left side, cut through that room, and then open the door exactly opposite. Then right till it ends, then right again, and the apprentice wing will be the second door on that hall." Eimin gave a wave. "Now go, I am busy. Scholar Dolomin has given me some research to do, and a lowly just-here apprentice is not anything I need or want to get in my way."

Layten walked away, rolling his eyes. He was thankful that the fool couldn't see his face, just the back of his head. The hall ended at a statue of some man holding a dagger. The man was thin, almost gaunt, and the dagger was jet black. Layten found it unnerving but took a right as he'd been directed. Four doors later, on the left, was an unmarked door that had seen use, but not recently it appeared. A thin layer of dust, the first he'd seen in this place, clung to the door handle.

The only reason he knew it had been used, though, was the floor. Marks from the opening and closing had etched themselves into the flagstones, marks that take thousands of openings over a great many years to make. So, someone used it, or had used it. The door handle felt strange to Layten; it seemed to be cold to the touch, but almost made his fingers burn. He jerked his hand away, but the door opened with the movement.

Layten looked around, but Eimin was nowhere to be seen. He was suspicious now of the directions he'd been given. But he WAS lost. Did he just wander around and hope to find someone else or by random chance the way back to his room? Or did he continue on? The room beyond wasn't dark, and before deciding, he was curious, so he stepped in.

It was obvious what the room was as soon as he did so. It was a small temple to Sartum. Rows of benches and a few grander chairs filled the space. There was a thin layer of dust still though, everywhere. He wondered about that until he realized that without the students of the House of Knowledge, the room wasn't getting much use. Soon enough the room would be clean and used again.

The knowledge made his jaw unclench. Maybe he'd misjudged Eimin somewhat. The man was still pompous and a fool, but he wasn't trying to hurt Layten. Maybe he was just one of those who lashes out at others to hide their own fears. His father had hired one man like that once. He acted the whole season like he knew more than anyone about reed beds, and making paper, and dealing with the marshes, and everything else.

The man had known some things, but nothing anyone who had worked a season or two wouldn't know. His mother, who liked everyone, had found him not worth her time to even talk to. Yes, Eimin was just like that. The idea made him feel sorry for the fool. Not quite able to make Scholar, living here because he had no other purpose, and lashing out at those he found a threat. Why Layten was a threat he didn't know. He wasn't.

The door behind him closed with a solid thunk, breaking his musing. He looked around and saw the opposite door, and quickly made his way towards it, only to stop as a new sound came. The sound of metal dragging across stone and more metal. Almost a tinkling sound, it grew louder, and Layten could tell where it was coming from.

He turned towards the altar, to see something he'd never expected to see. A giant mechanical thing, half legs, almost like a spider, but the other half, the back half, looked more like a scaled snake. That was where the scraping sound was coming from as the metal scales dragged across the stone floor, and each other as they curled up. The thing was coming from the ceiling, which Layten just realized he couldn't see. Everything faded into a jet-black void, giving the impression that if you could jump high, you'd just fall upwards, forever. Layten knew what this was. It was a guardian. A relic of the fall of the City. The great god Sartum had made a handful of the creations after that ancient war. Each one set to guard a special place. Given life through the power of the God, they were powerful and merciless. In the war of the joining, one had wiped out almost all the Army of Filo. Granted, Filo had been a small country, but still, just one of these things had wiped them all out in a single day. A now somewhat familiar feeling of icy cold and emptiness filled Layten. He hated it, but it was obvious that anything dealing with magic made him feel this way. The thing approached Layten, who realized why Eimin had sent him this way. This thing, this guardian, was going to end Layten's life. He knew it. The apprentice got lost, he wandered like a fool, and ended up someplace he should have never been alone. That was it. What a fool Layten had been to feel any pity for Eimin. His hands were clammy now, and sweat was already beading on his forehead. He was going to die. Right here. Right now. He wanted to run but couldn't. The sight of this thing, this mechanical beast, had him unable to move. Or maybe it was something else, he couldn't even move a finger.

The guardian was now fully descended from wherever it had been, and it was even larger than Layten had thought. It took up over half of the room, and to the small part of Layten who wasn't sure he was about to die, was surprised to see it carefully pick its way around the room, avoiding even brushing against any chairs or benches, or anything else.

"You should not be here." The voice was strange. If anything, it sounded like lute strings, plucked hard, but making a voice all the same. "This place isn't for you." Layten swallowed, his throat now dry. "I am sorry." He managed to croak out.

"You should not be here. This is not your place." The guardian lowered its head to be even with Layten. Its head was nearly the size of Layten himself. Four greenish and blue globes reflected the image of Layten back at him. A spark of light moved in those globes. *Eyes? Maybe?* Layten was caught up in his fear, but also his curiosity. "I will leave." He finally said.

"This is the wrong place for you. I can see it." The guardian rose up. "You are not of here."

Layten had no idea what that meant, but wasn't going to argue or ask questions, even if he wanted to know. Not now. He found he could move now, and he intended to do so. He shuffled towards the far door, watching as the guardian watched him. It said nothing more but kept those four globed eyes locked onto him. Making it to the door, Layten gave it a pull, afraid for a moment that it would be locked or barred, but it slid open without a sound and Layten pushed his way through the small opening, keeping his eyes on the guardian the whole time, until he could close the door, safe at last.

Layten slumped to the floor. The fear now gone, his body gave up on him for now. Sweat cooled and beaded up, falling down his face and drawing a few blinks. Eimin had set him up, he was sure of it. He was just very thankful that for whatever reason the guardian had let him go. Maybe it knew he had been tricked into coming there. *The wrong place for you.* That temple had been that, indeed. At least for now.

He wondered for a moment when the full session actually started, and if they all had to go there, would he have the same reaction. Somehow, he doubted the guardian would in fact even be seen. No, it must have known somehow that he'd been tricked and let him go. It was made by a God after all. It was special. The idea of magic being used, while uncomfortable, didn't quite have the same sting as it usually did. Layten wondered if he was getting used to the idea, if reluctantly.

It was one thing to read that the magic, the power, was evil, unless it was a gift from Sartum, and another thing fully to experience it. That was the whole issue. He had been sheltered so long on the coast. The Marsh. His parents. Layten smacked his head; he'd forgotten to talk to Scholar Dolomin or Scholar Nimer about how to get a letter back home.

His mouth set into a thin line before he gave a laugh for himself. Maybe it was better he'd forgotten. He was sure Eimin would have made note of it. The next time he could talk to one of them without 'Senior Journeyman Eimin Galantine' around, he'd ask. He could write the letter now though. Assuming he could get back to the right hall.

Much to his surprise, the rest of Eimin's instructions were correct, and soon he was back where he was supposed to be. He stripped off his now sweat-stained robes and relaxed for a moment. It had been one very interesting day. He wondered what the next day would bring.

Chapter Eighteen

Layten was bored. It had turned out that the next day brought nothing interesting. Nor the next after that. At least not in terms of the levels of excitement and sometimes terror the other days had brought. He had gotten his answer about getting a letter home the next morning. A simple affair of just putting the letter in a designated satchel for that land. The satchels were checked twice a week. It turned out the House of Knowledge sent a great many letters, books, and scrolls out into the world. Which made sense.

The satchels were in a long rectangular room by the stables. While students or at least apprentices did not bring their own horses, the House had a fair number of the animals and some scholars and journeymen had them as well. It was here that Layten finally met someone who worked here as staff. A pale woman, who wore greenish gray leathers with hair as dark as anything he'd ever seen. He found it almost hard to look at as the strands flowed into one another but never seemed to reflect any light. She had nodded to Layten when he appeared but said nothing.

Scholar Nimer explained later to Layten when he'd asked, the foresworn never spoke to anyone who wasn't one of their own. It was some agreement with Sartum himself. Curiously to Layten, no one knew what the agreement entailed, but anyone who tried to find out never did. It wasn't considered a polite thing to even talk about, as both the Scholars on staff right then attempted to change the subject as soon as he brought it up.

So now, Layten was bored. He only had access to the small apprentice study, and its plethora of books on subjects that did not interest him. He'd spent most of this morning looking for the most esoteric research he could find and had unearthed a seven-month study of the stiffness of pastry cream when cross referenced with phases of the moons.

But he knew he wasn't going to be bored much longer, and that idea helped him through this part. Tomorrow the staff arrived back, and the day after the House of Knowledge would officially allow students to enter. Layten knew that the only reason he'd been let it early was because of his father's relationship with this place, and he was grateful for it.

He had taken a short walk outside the House when he realized that it wasn't against the rules. For an hour it had been exciting, and then he realized just how expensive everything was. He'd gone to an inn and been taken aback by the pricing. Rooms were even going for a single silver a night. He only had three silvers to his name, and a dozen Lowter bronze bits. If the House hadn't let him in, he'd be living on the street while he waited.

Well, his father's connections and the Anchors had saved him from that fate. He'd tried very hard to not think about all that oddness. Everything that had happened during the short time he'd traveled with the Anchor and the Protectors. And he couldn't even talk about it. Or at least did not want to talk about it. Not that there was anyone to discuss it with right now. But it didn't matter, that was behind him. He was going to be a Scholar. That was what mattered.

For now, he wondered what his roommates would be like. Layten had been an only child, and since he'd grown up in the marshlands with just his parents, he'd never had close friends his own age. He'd interacted some with children from the village, but only if he was there with his father or mother. By the time he'd gotten old enough to do the trip on his own, what few children the village held wanted nothing to do with the strange boy who lived outside of town. So, he'd played when he was younger with one or two others just a few times. Living with two other young scholars was going to be interesting. He wondered what they would be like. Where would they be from?

He'd know soon. But the constant waiting had gnawed at him some. He'd avoided being anywhere near Eimin alone since that day. The man had looked somewhat annoyed to see Layten the next morning after the whole temple incident. Layten for his part had debated about saying something to Scholar Dolomin but had decided against it. He hoped by letting it all go he'd smooth things over and they could just stay out of each other's way. He hoped.

He was stretched out on his bed, flipping through the book on Protector fighting forms when a knock on the door came, surprising him enough that he dropped the book on the floor in his haste to get up.

The door swung open to reveal a tall young man around Layten's age. He was accompanied by two other men, who carried packs on their backs and a very large trunk between them. The younger man gave Layten a long appraising look and the room a glance. A resigned glance at that. He took a large breath and then shrugged.

"Fine. Put it all over there." He pointed the bed by the washroom area. The two men with him placed the packs and trunk by the bed before going out into the hall. The young man joined them for a moment and then they left, leaving Layten wondering just who this man was. It was obvious he was a roommate, but what was he doing here now?

The new roommate finally reentered the room and looked around again. "Austere." He finally said before walking over to Layten. "I am Hopwell. Hopwell Linew. Technically Golon Hopwell Linew." He extended a hand towards Layten.

Layten searched his memory; he'd heard the title Golon before. It was a mid-level nobility title from… Buniler. Buniler was a country in the Northeast. Rocky coastlines, lots of trees. Lots of mining as well. He realized that the man was still waiting with a hand outstretched and looked annoyed at Layten ignoring it. "Oh, sorry!" Layten gave him a firm handshake. A handshake is a measure of a man. Some trader had told him that. Said that he'd never trust a man who didn't give him a good handshake. "Layten Grayread. From Lowter." He almost instantly regretted saying Lowter, as every time he mentioned it, he got jokes and cracks about being form poor dirty Lowter.

Thankfully this Hopwell just nodded. "Lowter. Never been there. Never met anyone FROM there. I see we will be roommates this year? Who is the other bed for I wonder?"

"No idea. I wasn't expecting anyone else to be here until the day after tomorrow." Layten's lack of experience in this sort of communication was bothering him.

"Yes. I wasn't expecting anyone to be here either."
Hopwell arched a single eyebrow for a moment before
looking around again. "How are you here so early?"
"Oh well… the people I left Lowter with left earlier
than expected and got here faster. To be honest, I only
was let in because my father does a lot of business with
the House here." Layten thought about the Anchor
again but let it go. Why mention something that might
make this potential new friend think poorly of him?
"Oh? What does your father do?" Hopwell turned to his
bed and had already begun to unpack. Right away
Layten noticed a few things. One, everything he put
away was of very high quality. And two, some of it was
… strange for the House of Knowledge. A rich blue and
silver doublet? That's the colors of the House of Song.
And a small harp as well.
"He's a papermaker. We supply, well, my parents
supply the finest paper to the House of Knowledge and
across the North." Layten felt embarrassed saying that
to an actual noble.
"Oh?" Hopwell turned around and gave Layten a more
careful appraisal. "You dropped your book."
Layten turned around and spied the book on the ground,
its pages open. He picked it up carefully, brushing it
off. "Thanks, your entrance surprised me."
"Not a problem." Hopwell raised his head trying to see
the cover. "What book is that?"
"Oh, it's a book of Protector formal battle practices. I…
um... acquired it on my way here. I was told to keep it
as Protectors don't use any of these anymore." Layten
put it on the desk behind him.
"Really? May I see it? It might be useful, preparing me
for next year." Hopwell paused. "But not now, I must
focus on this."

"What do you mean next year?" Layten was puzzled by the comment.

"My father is a traditionalist. All young Golon used to go through what we call the rounding. Hardly any nobles do anymore, but my father insisted. Rounding is where we spend one year in each House. A year at the House of Song, a year here at the House of Knowledge, a year at the House of Blood, and so on. Five houses, five years." Hopwell shrugged. "Then we become part of the official court."

"Oh!" Layten had never heard of this. But it explained the doublet and harp. "Let me guess you just came from the House of Song." Layten pointed to the harp. "and now you are here, then off to House of Blood."

"Exactly." Hopwell picked up the harp, giving it a strum. The notes seemed to dance around the room, breaking the somber edge the air here always seemed to have. "I don't know if the book will be of any use, but if anything, it might help keep me in shape. I fear being a Scholar for a year may make it that much harder for me next year at drills and fighting."

Layten felt a twinge of annoyance at that comment but wasn't sure why. Hopwell wasn't saying anything that wasn't true. Layten had felt a bit soft since getting here himself. He was used to the workshop and moving heavy bales of reeds around or moving large stacks of pulp and paper. Or emptying innumerable barrels of water. He'd not done any of that for over a week now, and he felt softer.

"I may join you, at least to stay in better shape." Layten gave a smile. He liked this Hopwell, he thought. And he wanted the man to like him.

"If you like." Hopwell shrugged and went back to unpacking.

"When you are done, I'll show you the supply room. You get your apprentice robes and kit there. In a few bells we eat. From what I understand the vast majority of the staff return tomorrow, and the students officially return the day after that." Layten leaned back against his desk trying to decide if Hopwell's detached mannerisms were just a product of his imagination, or just one of those things that nobles do.

In truth he was the first noble that Layten had ever met. Lowter only had a small handful of nobles, and a self-proclaimed 'Water Lord' who dwelled in its capitol, Jutre. Layten had never been there, and no one he knew had ever been there either. The only contact they ever had with anyone even related to that was the tax collector who came by once a year. And even he just turned over his collections and ledgers to someone else who took it to the capitol.

Hopwell took his time unpacking, but not really talking to Layten, to Layten's annoyance. The man had more things with him than Layten had ever owned in his life. A thick book of music joined some of the other items from the House of Song that he'd put on his bookshelf. Nearly a dozen various items of clothing, most marked with what Layten assumed was his family sigil. An animal of some kid, wielding a rapier, with a red bar behind it.

Layten knew there was a whole class devoted to family sigils here at the House of Knowledge, and he wondered if that was something he'd take this year. His questions about his first year had often been deflected by the two Scholars he'd interacted with. Usually with a comment about needing to wait until the year actually began.

"All right. Show me what I have to have." Hopwell pushed his trunk over to one side, its weight still obvious, even now. He'd not taken anything out of it other than a few items of clothing, and it was clear it was still very full.

"Right this way. It will be time to eat soon as well, I can introduce you to the few staff that are here now. Assuming they are all there." Layten beckoned Hopwell to follow.

Chapter Nineteen

Hopwell tugged at his robe a few times, frowning. "Ridiculous things." He waved an arm, the extra cloth fluttering. "All it's going to do is get in the way." "Of what?" Layten after a day or two had found he rather liked the robes. The House of Knowledge was colder than he was used to, and they were warm. "Well, of writing, for one. I think it would be pretty easy to smudge ink with all this extra material." Hopwell attempted to roll the sleeve up some, or at least fold it in. Both failed.

"Ink. Oh yes. Dinner. At dinner there's a good bet Scholar Nimer and Scholar Dolomin will be there. Scholar Nimer is the Scholar of the First Gate, Dolomin is the Scholar of the Second Gate. I'm not sure exactly what that means. There's also often a very annoying man named Eimin. He's a Senior Journeyman. I think that means he keeps failing at making Scholar, and he's…" Layten shrugged.

"It means he's an angry and bitter man. I'm a noble, Layten, I see bitter and angry people all the time. Men, women, doesn't matter. Anyone who thinks they deserve something and don't get it, they all end up the same." Hopwell frowned one last time at his sleeve. "I still think these things are worthless. But... I am hungry."

"Well then right this way. This place is a maze." Layten thought about telling him about the temple and its guardian but wondered if that would seem like bragging. Hopwell was quite unlike any idea of a noble he'd ever had. And he got the feeling that bragging to him would be a mistake.

"There's one other person who might be there. Well, one other Trinil. He was there the first day, but not afterwards." Layten led Hopwell through the halls, feeling much more confident of how to get around. A minor victory, but one he enjoyed.

"A Trinil? Here?" Hopwell stopped and frowned. "How? Why?"

"I had the same question. According to him, Master Retuin, that is, there are a dozen or so Trinil that now follow Sartum. I had never heard such a thing. There's the long Gorom who helps get people to the gate, Waiter-in-the-Halls. But a Trinil?" Layten paused. "Did you meet Waiter-in-the-Halls?"

"No. We came a different way. A Gorom makes sense, at least somewhat. But a Trinil?" Hopwell shook his head. "What does he do here?"

"He's the ink maker. He wasn't forthcoming much about what he did." Layten shivered, just for a moment. "He was, strange."

"Trinil are. My father has had dealings with a merchant who is a Trinil. Captain Ser'Fal. He's a… wine trader." Hopwell smiled. "We like wine, and the south has better wine than we do. By far."

"That's allowed?" Layten was surprised. Trade, with the south? "What If they try to poison you, or worse?" Hopwell laughed. "Layten, these are merchants. They just want to make money. North or south, the only thing a merchant cares about is the sound in his money purse at the end of the day. And to trade with the free lands, he has to pay a hefty price. He wouldn't want to lose that trading license."

Layten knew that much to be true. His father had once said some of the traders who came to their workshop would sell their own families, if they could get a good enough profit. It just felt odd, the idea of trading with the south. "Well Master Retuin hasn't been at dinner since the first day I was here. I'm not sure why." Hopwell seemed to consider this and smiled, gesturing Layten to lead on. "Is the food good here at least? In the House of Song there're so many restrictions and rules on eating and drinking. Which food might cause some extra phlegm, which drink might make you have to interrupt a performance. It's exhausting."

Layten filed that away for later. He'd never thought of that. "Not that I'm aware. It's so far been simple food but well-made. There are cooks and the like, but they are part of some group called the forsworn. They don't talk to anyone who isn't a forsworn. Not a single word. I tried but was warned off."

"Don't worry, the same group exist at the House of Song. I imagine they exist at all the Houses. Pale? Dark straight hair?" Hopwell almost laughed. "Not unattractive, but hard to get to know, right?"

Layten smiled but didn't answer. As little experience he had with friends, he was even worse when it came to women. The whole idea of dating someone made him feel flustered and unsure of himself. "Oh yes." He finally said to fill the silence. "And here we are." He'd never been happier to see a door.

Layten pushed it open to see some changes had been made. The long tables up at the far end of the room had been setup. Four long tables, and each table now had fifteen chairs at them. Thick sturdy things they were padded though, and Layten realized that they must be setup for the returning staff.

The small table they had been eating at was still there. But only occupied by Scholar Nimer. No one else was in sight. They made their way over, hungry. Scholar Nimer looked up and smiled, seemingly pleased to see them.

"Ah, it's our two early arrivals. Apprentice Grayread and Apprentice Linew. I'm afraid it's a small dinner today, both in food and in company." Scholar Nimer waved them down across from her. "Soup, bread, and some kigil tarts."

Layten had no idea what a kigil was, but if it tasted as good as it already smelled, he would be fine with it.

"That's fine, Scholar Nimer." He lowered his head in respect. "I'm sure everything will be wonderful, company included."

"Flattery, young apprentice, will get you only so far… but it will get you somewhere." Scholar Nimer gave them both a warm smile. "Eat."

"Scholar Nimer, why is there a Trinil here?" Hopwell asked very offhandedly as he ladled soup into his bowl. "And while Layten here may have believed the story of their being twelve Trinil who follow Sartum, I do not. The records back home would have shown that."

The silence that fell over the table was obvious. Scholar Nimer put her spoon down and gave Hopwell a look that would have split him down the middle if he'd been paying attention. Layten was shocked that he wasn't. In fact, he finished putting his soup in his bowl and grabbed a roll and sat down with a smile.

"Apprentice Linew. That is House Scholar business. I will say this. The Church of Sartum knows and approves. That is all you need to know about any of it." Nimer stood and walked away, her back straight as if she was marching off to war.

"What by the blessed blood was that??" Layten kept his voice low and glanced around, making sure that Eimin was not lurking nearby. "What do you mean by questioning a full Scholar?"

"They were lying to you. Scholars should not lie." Hopwell ate some of the soup and frowned at it. "This needs salt."

"You don't go questioning a Scholar though! Not like that." Layten found himself not that hungry now. "What did you mean by the records back home?"

Hopwell put his spoon down and gave Layten an apprising look. "You really don't know do you? Buniler is where the Church of Sartum keeps its records. All its records."

Layten didn't know that. And it bothered him. "But why not here? At the House of Knowledge?"

"That, my friend, is a very good question. No one knows. Or at least no one who does know ever says. Same thing in the end." Hopwell looked around. "Do they not have salt to use?"

Layten found his nonchalant attitude about all this both impressive and annoying. Layten would have been a shaking mess of nerves. "But why question her?"

Hopwell just smiled. "I wanted to know why they were lying. Don't worry, I got my answer."

Layten had no idea now what Hopwell meant. "Well, you certainly haven't made a friend with her."

"Nonsense. If anything, once the shock wears off, Scholar Nimer will be far more willing to bend the rules or look the other way for minor infractions now. She left the table after I questioned her. She REALLY doesn't want anyone to ask those questions. So, she left rather than argue. She's scared she might say the wrong thing." Hopwell sopped up the last dregs of his soup and grabbed a tart. "What exactly is a kigil?"

"I don't know." Layten wondered at Hopwell's idea. It made sense in a strange way. There was no possible way Layten would ever try it though. It must be one of those things that only nobles can get away with. Layten took his own tart and sniffed it. "Smells fine."
One bite brought back some of his appetite. The crust was buttery and rich, and the kigil turned out to be some kind of nut, it appeared. But a nut that tasted of browned butter and exotic spices. It was quite good.
"Good," Layten managed to mumble without spitting crumbs all over the table.
Hopwell ate his own tart with relish. "Yes, it is. I'll have to remember that name."
Layten and Hopwell soon finished the tarts and Layten decided he was hungry now after all and quickly downed a bowl of soup. His stomach wanted another tart, but he stopped himself. No reason to be a glutton. "The question is then if the Trinil isn't supposed to be here, why is he and where is he?" Layten tapped the table, trying to think. "Master Retuin stared at me the whole time, at least after he learned who my father was."
"Well, part of that I will guess an answer to. He's not been here because of you. It's the same reason that Scholar left. When someone wants to hide something, and you ask about it, one of two things is going to happen. Either they will stay and fight, or they will leave you and avoid any chance, as best they can, that the subject comes up again." Hopwell pointed in the direction the Scholar went. "I'd lay my harp that somewhere in that direction your Trinil, this Master Retuin, is in a room right now, either eating or talking to the Scholars."

"So, the whole ink thing was fake?" Layten frowned. That didn't make sense to him. The interest the Trinil had shown in his father's work was real, not faked. "No, I didn't say that. He may very well be the ink maker for the House. There's just more going on. I doubt strongly that whatever it is, they expected two apprentices to ask questions. During the year no one would dare. And I don't think this Master Retuin ever interacts with students, at least far from often. I'd guess some other Scholar teaches ink making, and almost no one ever knows this Master is even here." Hopwell leaned back in thought. "The idea of being one of twelve Trinil who follow Sartum is a good deflection."
"And I fell for it," Layten added on.
"Yes and no. You recognized this was unusual. If I had not known the records, I would have accepted that version of the truth as well." Hopwell smiled. "Don't worry, Layten. Tomorrow is another day. The day after that our other roommate comes and then the real work begins."

Chapter Twenty

Anchor Fean thumped the table for the umpteenth time. Things were not good. He, Wilk and Binin had arrived back at the Anchorhold just three days ago, and the news he had gotten everywhere was terrible. Fourteen other recorded events of magical creatures being in the North. And not just a random sighting, but actual interactions that required an Anchor to be involved. Fourteen in a single month.

And then there were the missing Anchors. Besides the discovery of Anchor Nolmin, who never should have even been near that location, there were seven other known dead Anchors. Seven. And three more whose location was unknown. Worse yet, it appeared some of the dead had been… experimenting. Breaking the rules of their God, breaking the natural and proper order. They had tried to USE magic.

The fact that they had all died was a good thing. The mere idea or hint of an idea that an Anchor could possibly use magic, outside the blessing of Sartum, of course, would be cataclysmic to the order. Almost no one liked the Anchors at the best of times. They were hated, feared, and still yet loved for their service. But if the common folk ever got the message that the Anchors were using magic outside of Sartum's gifts, that thin thread of love would vanish.

Fean had managed to keep it quiet, at least for now. He had leaned heavily on Wilk and Binin once more to suppress all talk of that part of the deaths. He couldn't hide the rest of it but keeping that small piece out of the puzzle kept the order safe, at least for now. It wouldn't last; there was only one thing all this activity would lead to.

Fean could hear the screams sometimes, the wailing, the gibbering laughter of a thousand souls, the Anchors and their Protectors who had made the descent. He was close to it himself. Another thing he could not hide. He'd caught the whispers and looks when his left hand had been spotted. Already factions in the Anchorhold had formed, ready to position their favorite for advancement, once Fean took his descent. But he wasn't there yet.

In a few weeks the Priests and the Lords of the North would come. He would be duty bound to tell them what had been going on. He would not entrust that to anyone else, so he had to hold onto his sanity. He had to. Otherwise, it would be war.

Layten awoke to noise. A lot of noise. The day before, the whole place had been alive as a veritable army of Scholars, staff and Journeymen had descended on the House. He and Hopwell had made the mistake of leaving their room to see what was going on. In short order they had been put to work, carrying boxes and crates full of books, scrolls, maps, and whatever else. Most looked like they hadn't been touched in years. They had bounced around to whomever needed two strong backs and firm hands. At the end they had both decided to make haste elsewhere and retreated back to the Apprentice wing. After a brief discussion, they hid out in the Apprentice study, convinced that if they had been in their room, someone might look for them there. Those fears had been proven correct as several times they heard knocks coming down the hall before hearing the door to this wing close. None came down to the study, a fact they both found slightly amusing. The place was known to be just that boring that no one wanted to go there.

That night they had snuck out enough to grab some food set up at a 'get it when you want it' table and retreated back to their room. A quick bite and then sleep. Sleep that now was gone. For today was the day the students returned.

"By the fires of Sartum…" Hopwell groaned. "Can they not be quieter?" Hopwell sat up for a moment before collapsing back into the bed. "No, I'm not getting up." Layten agreed. He was tired still, and sore. The only thing that would have gotten him out of bed was food, and it was going to be a while till the next meal. His eyes did move over to the free bed, however. Today was the day the final member of the trio would arrive. Layten rather wondered who they would be.

He and Hopwell got along rather well, he thought. Though the man showed his more privileged upbringing often. Layten wondered if this was just a thing that came with being a noble. You can say whatever is on your mind without fear or repercussions. Hopwell might just be an apprentice, but he was still a noble.

It probably didn't hurt that he was never going to be a scholar. He was just here for a single year, as part of this 'rounding' he had to undertake. The idea made sense to Layten, though it did again reflect the privilege that Hopwell lived in. Many young men and women strove very hard to get into a single House and failed. And here Hopwell got to go to each one.

More yells and laughs came from the hall, and more of their fellow students arrived. And some of those voices were decidedly feminine. Layten found the idea somewhat nerve-inducing. But Hopwell, he was sure Hopwell was looking forward to that particular fact. A good-looking young noble, who happened to already be trained, at least partially, by the House of Song? Layten didn't begrudge him of course, Hopwell was just too likable for that. A small, tiny part was still jealous, regardless.

"They aren't going to let us sleep, are they," Hopwell groaned again, taking his pillow and stuffing his face into it.

Just then the door opened, and there stood the thinnest, shortest man Layten had ever actually seen. "Oh… you must be my roommates," the man said.

Or at least that was what Layten thought he said. The way this man spoke was hard to understand. Each word was spoken at nearly a whisper, and at the same time, very quickly. Layten had to go over it a few times to make sure he understood. "Yes." He finally said, realizing the new member of their trio was still standing in the doorway. "I'm Layten Grayread. That is Hopwell Lewin."

"Excuse me? Golon Hopwell Lewin to you," Hopwell mumbled from his bed.

Layten smirked; he knew Hopwell enough now to know when he was being an ass on purpose. "Fine. GOLON Hopwell Lewin."

The new roommate blinked a few times. "Oh...a Golon. And someone from Lowter. How interesting. Why are you both already here? How long have you been here? Is that my bed? When do we eat?" The small man's words came flooding out, and Layten felt more like he was trying to skip the words like a stone on the water than actually say them.

"Well, you could tell us your name, and then we can go from there," Layten answered, trying to make sense of the barrage of questions.

"Name. Name would be good." Hopwell's agreement floated out of the pillow, if not slightly muffled.

"Oh, sorry my name is Wix. Wiximinon Quilit. From Ture." The small man gave a head bow and threw a single bag onto the free bed. "Done. When do we eat?"

"Wixim... Wix it is." Layten had never heard a name like that. Or honestly met anyone who spoke like that either. "You said Ture?"

"Yes. Ture. Born there." Wix's words rushed out. "You speak slow."

"And you speak oddly." Hopwell finally pushed himself up to a sitting position. "I've been to Ture. And I've never met anyone or talked to anyone who speaks like you there. Or anywhere."

"Parents are from far away. Very far. Lost at sea. Survived. Ended up in Ture. Had me." Wix shrugged. "Talk fine at home. You'll get used to it."

Layten hoped he had caught all that. He wondered where exactly Wix's family was from if they spoke like that. But that might be a question for another time when they all knew each other somewhat better. "He's right, Hopwell. We probably want to get ready and go get to breakfast before it becomes even more crowded there. And right after we have that introduction and class assignments, and all the rest. The days of sleeping in are over for a week."

"Yes, yes. Fine." Hopwell rubbed his hands over his face. "At least I will now have something better to look at than you while we eat."

It did not take long for them to get ready. Layten found himself rather excited the more he thought about it. Things were going to actually start happening. He could learn things, research things, dive into esoteric concepts and everything else that happens here. And he even liked his roommates. Wix was strange, at least a little, but nothing that gave Layten a bad feeling. And he genuinely liked Hopwell. The man had an instinctive ability to put people at ease. A useful skill for a noble to have.

"Well, are we going to wait here all day or go eat? I spend all morning prodding the two of you…."

Hopwell grinned and ducked the pillow Layten threw at him in response.

"Come on." Layten went first, followed by Wix and then Hopwell. Layten had to stop though and take note of everything going on.

The hall was chaos. Forty or more students were milling around, introducing themselves, talking and pointing. Roughly half were women and half were men. He got a few looks of curiosity, as did Hopwell. He didn't understand at first, then he realized they were wearing the apprentice robes. No one else was, not even Wix. They hadn't gotten them yet.

A smiling red-headed girl approached him first, sticking out a hand. "Delerie."

Layten looked at it for a moment, maybe a moment too long, as he heard Hopwell give an obviously fake cough behind him. Layten managed to recover and shook the offered hand. "Layten."

"Where did you get those robes that you and your friend are wearing?" Delerie asked, plucking one sleeve.

"They are the Apprentice robes. Hopwell and I got here early for various reasons, so we already have ours. I'm sure you will get them today." Layten tried to give her a confident smile. She was attractive, and she smelled… nice. Raspberries and… he couldn't place the other part.

"Oh? How long have you been here?" Delerie looked up, a smile on her face.

"About a week for me. Hopwell, a little less than that." Layten shrugged. "We were about to go eat. Wix here is hungry." Layten pointed at their new roommate, who nodded, but didn't seem all that interested in talking to this new person.

"May we join you? This place is confusing. They gave us a map but still…." Delerie waved over a dark-haired girl. "This is my roommate Talir."

Layten smiled at Talir but said nothing. The silence was getting awkward when he realized they were waiting for him to lead them on. "Follow me," he said and led the little group forward and out of the hall.

Chapter Twenty-One

Layten unclenched and clenched his hand, trying to make the cramping in his fingers more bearable. He was a month into his first year here at the House of Knowledge. And he was very much trying to put a happy face on it. To himself though, he was already questioning his own sanity for ever coming here.
Not that any of the Apprentices felt differently. Hopwell threw more than a few insults at several of the Scholars who taught them, at least in the privacy of their room. And Wix had tried to hide his tears one night this past week when his hand had literally cramped into place and refused to open.
"Layten. This hurts. Why do they make us do this?" Wix nodded at the papers in front of them. It was rote copying of older manuscripts that were starting to fall apart. Layten understood the reasons though. And he gave Wix a smile.
"We must improve our writing to Scholar Kof's liking." Layten kept his voice low, looking up briefly to see the Scholar where he usually was, behind a desk shaking his head and throwing hours of work away in a nearby fire and sending the apprentice back to their seat to start over.
Wix scowled. "He would not like anything."
"I agree. And could they at least give us something interesting to copy?" Hopwell picked up a corner of the paper he was working on, its age shown in thin edges and a dark yellow and green stain that covered half the page. "This is the crop report from four hundred years ago."

Layten knew what Hopwell meant. Layten had the theory that all this was designed to break them and see who the true Scholars could be. Hopwell had scoffed at the idea, and Wix had shrugged. "Better than starving on the streets." Wix seemed to always want to eat. Layten and Hopwell had tried multiple times to get the small man to share more of his past, but Wix seemed to always be on guard. The best they could tell was that his family had always been poor or was poor now. And that Wix had no other choice but to come after he'd been accepted. As for his odd manner of speech and his background, they were no closer to getting that from him. If they pressed, he simply shrugged and didn't answer.

"Burn this robe!" Hopwell threw down the marking pen he was using as ink spilled down, covering his work.

"Apprentice Lewin. What a surprise." Scholar Kof got up from his desk with a stretch.

Layten found Kof to be unsettling. He wore his full Scholar robes, and even then, he looked thin. Without the robes the man must be more skeleton than anything else. Skin, tight against the bones of his face, made every expression odder looking than the last.

Layten would have been fine with that; he wasn't going to be overly harsh on a thin old man after all. But adding in the way he moved, like an insect stalking its prey, and it just made him feel…unnatural. As if the man was about to lash out and stab him with a pointed finger. Just like the long sharp finger he was now pointing at Hopwell.

"You have ruined your work, Apprentice Lewin. You had better hope you did not damage the work you were copying." Scholar Kof tapped the desk Hopwell was working on with that one finger. "Your outbursts are also disturbing the others."

Hopwell for a moment seemed to be chastised. But Layten knew his friend and didn't think it would last. Hopwell was nothing if not sure of his convictions, and he made very sure everyone knew it.

"It's these blasted robes. These sleeves are wrong. They just get in the way. Not to mention how dull and frankly time-wasting copying these papers are anyway. You want us to have better handwriting? Fine, teach it. But just having us do copying work that has no point other than wasting our time, is ridiculous." Hopwell nearly yelled the words, crossing his arms as he spoke and ignoring the large ink stain that now covered those same robe sleeves.

"Ohhh?" Scholar Kof's voice rose to a dry note, like someone blowing air across a bottle top. "I see our little lordling here thinks he's above this. Well, little lordling, this is the way the House of Knowledge has always done it. We use this to weed out those who can't make it. You think being a Scholar is easy? Simple? No! It requires years of dedication. Decades of knowledge and pursuing the truth. Did your father have a Scholar?" Kof asked, taking a small step back from Hopwell's desk, and the ink that had now managed to spill onto the floor and was gathering in a small black pool.

"Yes." Hopwell frowned as the admission came.

"I would imagine so. And did that Scholar ever tell your father he didn't know something? Was ever unable to help?" Scholar Kof pressed the fingers of both hands together, awaiting Hopwell's answer.

"No." Hopwell started to say something else but stopped.

"Exactly. Being a Scholar is HARD. You must be able to answer any question put to you. And know it to be true. This room, here, is not to improve your writing." Scholar Kof looked around, seeing all the Apprentices looking up now. "This is to prove your dedication. To prove to the House of Knowledge that you will do ANYTHING to be of service to our way of life. Free of the taint of uncontrolled magic. Devotion to Sartum. Strength and resolve in the face of a southern foe that wishes to destroy everything we have or have ever built.

"And that is why we are here, little lordling. I know you are not here as a normal apprentice. You do not have to dedicate your life to anything, other than being a noble. No great sacrifices would ever be called upon for you. Maybe that is why this is hard for you? Because it requires you to sacrifice. Something you have never had to do?" Scholar Kof gave a smile as sharp as a shaving razor.

Hopwell did not look sorry now. Angry was more like it. Layten could see his friend about to blow up when Wix saved the day.

"Scholar. We understand. Dedication is a good thing." Wix smiled, his quiet, fast words interrupting the tension, and giving just enough diffusion for Hopwell to realize this wasn't a fight he was going to win, at least not right here or now.

"As Wix says," Hopwell mumbled and lowered his face.

"Excellent. Now, clean this up, Apprentice Lewin. And start over. You cannot leave until you are done." Scholar Kof gave another one of his thin tight smiles and sat back behind his desk, ignoring them all once more.

Layten and Wix waited out in the largest hallway for Hopwell to appear. The hall had sort of become the place where students met and talked. It was odd that it wasn't the hall where their rooms are, but here, just a somewhat random hall that just happened to be large enough for most to congregate.

"Hopwell got very angry. Angry indeed." Wix paced back and forth, shaking his head. "That was foolish. Very foolish."

"Well, he had some reason. You agree that all that copying work is rather…." Layten held up his writing hand, still slightly curved as if was still holding his pen.

"Oh yes. But he must do better controlling anger. We are just people. But he is a noble." Wix sighed. "He is the only noble I have ever met though. Maybe it is more common for nobles to get angry?"

"I wouldn't know," Layten shrugged. At least there was something worth paying attention to while they waited. Not that he didn't like talking to Wix. He liked Wix. Wix was…different. Smart, fast, and able to read a room quite well. The main thing that held him back from being more popular around the House was the way he spoke. He was just so hard to understand.

But out here, Delerie was talking to her roommate and another girl named Erim. Delerie, he had learned, was from a village in Orbask, near the Jolum mountains. Which explained the slightly accented way she spoke. Everything had a slight upward tilt to it. Hopwell rolled his eyes at the sound, but to Layten it just added to his attraction.

It was of course at that exact moment that Delerie noticed him watching her. She smiled and gave a slight head nod, which in turn made Layten lower his head and try to look anywhere else.

"You like that girl, Delerie?" Wix had noticed of course. Wix always noticed.

"Yes." Layten wasn't going to lie. "But I don't… I don't know what…well you know."

"Ah. Yes. You grew up on the marshlands, in Lowter. No girls. Very sad for you." Wix laughed. "Girls are wonderful. They make you feel better when they smile at you, they smell wonderful, and the touch of their skin…."

"Stop please," Layten interrupted Wix. "That's the last thing I need in my head right now."

Wix slapped him on the back. "Do not worry. She is still smiling at you. This means she likes your fear and uncomfortable look right now. She likes you."

Layten groaned. Wix and Hopwell had far more knowledge than him about women, and it showed. Wix had spent a lot of time with one tiny girl down the hall who was even shorter than he was. Luiy her name was. And Hopwell?

True to what Layten had expected, Hopwell had already had a half dozen entanglements in the month since everything had started. Noble, rich, smart, and thanks to his time already in the House of Song, somewhat trained in the harp and he had a surprisingly rich singing voice. The first week, no more than five different women had knocked on their room door looking for Hopwell. Often when he was off pursuing some other conquest.

"I truly hate that man." Hopwell's voice brought Layten back to the here and now.

"And it was obvious he does not like you. But you must control your anger." Wix almost sounded like he was scolding Hopwell.

Hopwell sat down by them on a chair they had left for him. "I've been scrubbing ink off that stone floor for nearly a bell. I don't want to even look at ink for the rest of the day. No writing." He closed his eyes and leaned back, sinking into the chair.

"You know I'd never heard that before, Hop. About nobles having a Scholar as an advisor." Layten didn't want to think about Delerie, and at least Hopwell wouldn't needle him about his fears.

"It used to be more common. A lot more common. My father is old-fashioned, you know, like with this rounding? He also has a Scholar. Scholar Rieb Tillow. I assume he was useful, once. These days he's so old he can barely hear." Hopwell rubbed his eyes. "I am so sick of reading. I'm getting soft here. When this term is over, I have to go to the House of Blood, and at this rate I'll be plumper than a baker's apprentice."

Layten had noticed that he'd put on some weight as well. A lot less physical work here than at the workshop, and the food was richer. An idea tickled his mind. "Hey, that book I have. The one of Protector training. Well, old training."

"You have a book on Protector training?" Wix looked up surprised. "I did not know this."

"Sorry, I got it on my way here. Long story." Layten still hadn't told either of them about his strange trip with the Anchor and his Protectors. Though if he waited much longer, they might be annoyed at him for keeping it from them.

"What about it?" Hopwell raised his head.

"We could do the exercises. They aren't worth anything in terms of real fighting training I know. But at least it's exercise, right?" Layten rubbed his chin with a thumb. "I looked through it a few times. Basic exercises for strength and agility. And then sword forms, spear forms, and archery techniques. We can't do all of it, but it's something different than our normal work."

"That, my Lowter friend, is a grand idea." Hopwell was sitting up, looking far more pleased than when he'd sat down. "You care to join us, Wix?"

"Might be interesting. Yes, indeed, interesting." Wix nodded. "I am in too."

Chapter Twenty-Two

Layten jumped back, swinging his 'sword' in a low arc, trying to bat away Hopwell's attack. Of course, his sword was nothing more than a length of wood, but at least it was round and fairly solid. Hopwell's attack was made of the same thing. And the wood hit with a solid crack. Wix was sitting back, already exhausted from today's sparring and practice.

They had been at it now for roughly a month. Every day for a bell or two, depending on the day and what else was going on. At first Layten had hated it. He'd been sore, tired, and badly regretted even bringing the idea up. Hopwell of course had loved every second of it, and convinced Layten and Wix, who also hated it, to continue. Now, they loved it just as much as Hop did. Wix had said it made the other work easier. After the first hurdle of just being sore was over with, he found it easier to concentrate. Layten agreed with him. And even doing some of the more formal battle 'dances' was helpful. Once he had learned them, he found it even relaxing to have his body doing those while his mind was free to concentrate on other things.

Usually, those other things involved research. After the outburst and argument with Scholar Kof, things had gone more smoothly. It wasn't even a week or two later when all of them were moved out of that class. Layten found it surprising, but Hopwell had just smiled. He never SAID he'd done anything, but he also did nothing to end the suspicion.

As a result, they had moved on to learning how to research something. At first Layten had wondered what the point was. You research, right? You read things, make notes and there you go. But most of the class was devoted to figuring out what exactly to read. Figuring out if what you had been reading was fake, was it full of opinion or fact? Opinion was important, sometimes, but you had better be able to figure out which was which.

Layten was good at it. Hopwell was not bad. Wix excelled at it. He claimed it was mostly because he had grown up around thieves and grifters. If you didn't learn quickly how to spot a lie, you might not make it through the night. Wix liked to argue with everyone about the truth, which made for an interesting class most of the time.

A stinging slap brought Layten back to the now. "Got you!" Hop laughed as he moved back three steps in a heel-to-toe line. "You're distracted, Lowter! Thinking about a red-haired girl?"

Layten frowned. "I was not. I wasn't distracted, I mean. Well, I was distracted but I wasn't thinking about…" he didn't get the words out before Hop lunged forward suddenly, the rounded point slamming into Layten's gut. "Ooooof," He managed to force out before he went down.

"Sorry, Layten!" Hop pulled Layten up. "You really do get distracted too easy sometimes. You need to concentrate on the here and now. Especially in a fight."

"I know." Layten rubbed where the point had hit him. "You're right."

"About the redhead?" Hopwell grinned at Layten's discomfort. "You keep leaving yourself open on that subject. You need to fix that."

"Yes." Wix chimed in. "We are friends, right? We are telling you. You like her. She likes you. This is not hard. The hard part is over with. Just see what happens now."

"Wix is right. Stop getting in your own way." Hopwell leaned on his 'sword.' "You aren't going to get anywhere pretending that you both just like each other as friends."

"I get it. Just... stop talking about it for right now?" Layten asked as the cold knot of fear and nerves in his gut grew with each prodding from his friends. They were right of course. He knew they were right. It was obvious that Delerie was interested in him. And he was more than interested in her. That would make it easier, right? But Layten found that made it all the harder, at least for him. And he seemed to be making Delerie somewhat annoyed with his lack of skill.

"Fine." Hopwell looked around the room. "It's a good thing we found this place. I wonder what it was used for."

Layten had found this room that they were using just last week. They had been looking for a new place to do the forms and training since it was cramped in their room. That and the fact that Layten had broken part of his desk with an errant thrust, and Wix had managed to slam the back of his head on the floor when he'd tripped trying to do a formal movement in too small a space.

The room he'd found was large, almost as large as the dining room. But it was empty other than an old rug that covered most of the floor, and half a dozen lamps, all covered with dust. That was it. It was strange that there was dust here as well. It seemed rooms that didn't get much use did get dirty after all. Layten found that comforting.

"I don't know. Maybe it had been a library at some point?" Layten looked around. "Though there's nothing on the carpet showing old shelf locations."

"I wish we had access to anything worth reading." Hopwell swung his wooden pole, the air swishing over it. "I spent two bells today reading the combined history of the rebirth of Amder."

"Very good. Though most of that is opinion." Wix added. "Truth mixed with lies. Harder to spot."

"What do you mean? It's all true. The turncoat one, that William Reis had with the blessing of Amder gathered the blood, hammer, and heart and with the help of the other traitor, remade Amder." Hopwell leaned against a stone wall. "They slew the High Priest and ripped the heart out of his dying hands."

"Partially true." Wix smiled. "You do not know."

"Well then, Wix, if you have all the answers... why don't you tell me what REALLY happened?" Hop's voice was edgier now.

Layten knew how much Hopwell disliked being wrong. He accepted it, but he didn't like it. And on this subject, he was sure he was right. Which of course just made Wix all the happier to show him the error. While they were friends, there was still a dynamic between them that never fully went away. Hopwell was a noble, born into privilege and power. Wix was a street kid, barely hanging on in his youth. Hopwell came from a long line of northerners. Wix's parents came from an unknown land. And of course, Hopwell was rich. Wix most decidedly was not rich.

But they usually did not let that one area of stark difference stand between them. At least not usually.

"Fine. I will show you. Show you both." Wix stood up with an undulation worthy of a snake. "But promise, no talking."

Hop looked confused for a moment and smiled. "You found a way into something, didn't you?"

"Yes. Very clever you are, Hop." Wix returned the grin. "Found a way into the special place. Into the fifth gate."

"There isn't a fifth gate. It only goes up to four," Layten pointed out. "Even the Head Scholar, Tinerus is the Master of the fourth gate."

"Ha!" Wix smiled. "You believe that? This place is old, Layten. Very old. Many nooks. Many rooms not entered in a long time. There is a fifth gate."

"Let's say you are right. You found a way in?" Hopwell put his shirt on and put his practice wooden sword into a corner. "I want to see this."

"There's no such place," Layten said again, but after seeing that both Wix and Hopwell weren't going to be dissuaded, he did the same as Hopwell, throwing a shirt back on and only wincing from what was sure to be a bruise on his stomach from that last blow from Hop. "Lead on with this folly," Layten grumbled.

Wix grinned and, putting on his shirt, led them through a series of turns and rooms that soon had them both confused and lost. "Do you actually know where you are going?" Layten asked as he realized he was lost beyond all hope.

"Oh yes. Mighty Sartum did many wonderful things here. One being the size of this place." Wix waved his arms. "Very large."

"How did you even find this supposed fifth gate?" Hopwell asked as they passed through a room that smelled of nothing but stale dead air and damp rot.

"I was looking for a place to spend time with Luiy. Away from you loud and nosey people," Wix answered as he pushed on a section of wall that as far as Layten could tell was just plain stone.

"Oh?" Hopwell perked up. "You will have to give me some ideas."

"Because the half of the women in the hall you haven't spent time with happen to be roommates with the half you HAVE spent time with," Layten snorted. "That would be awkward for you."

"I force no one to bask in my presence," Hopwell grinned. "You should take notes though, or maybe we should show Delerie, so she could get you moving."

"Shut it," Layten snapped back.

The wall slid back surprisingly quietly. Revealing a dark hall quite unlike any of the other hallways they had traveled through. Those had been paneled and decorated. Well-lit, too. This one was bare stone. The air was cold. Too cold. A cold he'd almost forgotten about.

For in front of them stood a door. A door with a smooth black orb embedded in it. An orb that if you looked at it writhed and flowed in patterns that made Layten's head hurt. A warding orb, he guessed? If that was even a thing that existed. He'd never seen one, if that was what it was. It gave him the same feeling as the warding circle at home. Or Anchor Fean's staff. That icy cold emptiness, a deep hunger. And the screams... faint, barely there, screams.

Chapter Twenty-Three

"Now that's something I've never seen." Hop walked towards the orb. "What is it?"

"It's a ward." Layten hated it on sight. His chest ached looking at the vile thing. "Can't you feel it?"

"Feel what?" Wix shrugged. "It's just a black stone." He led them past the door, down the hall, but not far. "Here." Wix pointed to a section of a corner that, to their surprise, was crumbling. Layten didn't know what to think.

He felt slightly better now that they were away from the orb directly, but that echoing cold emptiness still fell over him. He also did not like the idea that Hop and Wix didn't feel it. Why did he have that reaction, and they didn't? The questions that brought up were not ones he was ready to answer.

"That can't be." Hopwell pointed at the crumbling stonework. "All the Houses are the work of Sartum. Song, Blood, Knowledge, Craft, and Sail. Even the Anchorhold. They are creations of a God. They CAN'T crumble."

"Ah ha!" Wix grinned. "You are right, and you are wrong again, friend Hopwell. What you said is true, but as far as I can tell, this place, this fifth gate, was here before the House of Knowledge. How much longer I do not know. But this may be part of what was here before."

"Was there anything here before?" Layten hadn't considered this idea. "I never thought to explore the founding of the Houses. I only know that after the Great God returned from the destruction of the City, he then founded the Houses and the Anchorhold."

"Exactly." Wix was excited enough that his voice got even faster. "How long after did this happen? Which House was first? How did the Houses come to be what they are? Too many questions."

"Fine." Hopwell held up a hand to attempt to arrest the torrent of questions from Wix. "Let's say you are right, that this is from... whatever was here before Sartum formed the House. Why would you call it the fifth gate? That doesn't make sense."

Wix nodded. "To see that, you must follow." The man slid through the crumbling stone, into the room beyond. "And do not go towards the door from this side. You will understand."

Layten wasn't sure he or Hopwell would be able to squeeze through that broken masonry, but he was too far in now to back out. "I'll go next."

"Do so, if you can fit that Lowter bulk through. I know I'll make it." Hop grinned. He enjoyed needling Layten sometimes too much for Layten's tastes, but he knew Hop's heart was in the right place.

Layten got down on his knees and began to squeeze through the crack. The air was cold and very stale. The smell of dust and the faint smell of very old paper was carried with it. A small part of him wondered what the paper was like. Old habits die hard, he guessed. His shirt caught on a piece of broken stone, and tore, bringing a scratch and a wince as a thin line of red crossed both shoulder blades. But right after that he was free and standing in what to his eyes appeared to be a room that wasn't quite… right.

Hopwell managed to make it, without tearing his shirt. But he, too, stood there for a long moment, taking this strange new location into consideration. And strange it was. Layten turned in a circle trying to make sense of what he was seeing.

More than a dozen small tables were around them, each with a book or scroll upon them. That wasn't unusual. The room was lit with a greenish glowing light that was coming from the direction of that door they had passed. That was different, but not too much so. But the fact that the tables were floating, each about a boot's thickness above the floor, and the fact that the light came from a huge mechanical thing that was slumped over… that was strange.

"What is... that?" Hopwell pointed at the machine.

"Guardian," Layten whispered. "But… I've never seen one like that. Or read about one like that."

The one he'd seen before had been half-spider and half-snake. It had been designed to bring terror and awe to any who saw it. This was almost plain by comparison. If it hadn't been slumped over, it would have been as high as three grown men. It had four arms. Two huge ones, and two smaller ones. In the middle of the thing was a green globe, which was supplying the light here. It wasn't bright, but it worked. And the whole vast machine was balanced on a bronze metal-looking ball.

"Yes. Guardian." Wix pointed to the floating tables. "Protecting these."

Layten didn't like looking at the tables. Just another reminder of magic. But his curiosity about what could possibly be that important won out. "So, explain, Wix."

"These books. They are truth. What REALLY happened." Wix pointed to a book half open. "That is the true story of before the return of Sartum." He spun and pointed to a different book, this one yellow and closed. "And that is the truth of what happened before that, how the Sundered God came to be."

Hopwell snorted. "And you believe that?" He shook his head. "Wix, my friend, did it not occur to you that these books could be horrible lies and guarded by that thing to keep anyone from being exposed to them?"

"Ah. Yes." Wix waved them over to a bookcase that was not floating, and in fact was snug against the wall. It was hard to see in the dim green light, and Layten wouldn't have even noticed it if Wix hadn't pointed it out. On the top of it was small plaque. Not brass, but some other metal, inscribed with two things. The number five, and a name. A name they all knew. It was written in a very old style, but it was still clear.

"Jinir Yallow." Layten said the name slowly. "As in High Prophet Jinir?"

"Yes. This I think was his personal library." Wix waved his hands around. "Where he kept the truth."

"Why not take these books then and show them to the Scholars?" Hopwell's voice fell as he spoke.

Layten could see that his friend was far more unsure of himself than he had been just a few moments before.

"What would they do with it, I wonder?" he asked. He approached a beat-up leather-bound notebook. This one was tied with a simple blue cord.

"Ah. Well… watch." Wix walked over to a simple scroll and picked it up. Nothing happened until he moved it a few hands away from the table. Then the effect was immediate. The construct moved with silent grace so fast that Layten jumped back. The thing whirled around, outstretched claws at the end of each arm threatened to rip Wix apart. Wix, almost as fast, put the book back on its floating table and the Guardian returned to its slumber, slumping over again, and looking like it hadn't moved in generations.

"Can't take them. Can read them." Wix pointed to the tables. "So, I learn the truth. The greatest thing a Scholar can know."

"This is dangerous. Very dangerous," Hopwell frowned. "If we read these things, and say anything to anyone, the Priesthood may get involved. Or worse, the Chastisers."

"They don't exist anymore, Hop. You know that." Layten almost laughed at the suggestion, until he saw the faces of both Wix and Hopwell. "They can't exist!" The Chastisers had been an order that existed inside the Priesthood of Sartum back when the free lands were being unified. Finders of heresy, destroyers of lies. The stories about them made for great ways to scare children. They would drag anyone, lord, or commoner, rich or poor, out into the night and they were never seen again.

After the North had been more or less unified, Sartum had disbanded the order, proclaiming its goals fulfilled. And they hadn't been seen since. It was old history. It had to be.

"I do not know." Wix lowered his face. "I am from Ture. You know this. I grew up on the streets of Ture. You know this. Many times, I have seen people make a bad joke, or an insincere curse at Sartum, and in a day or two, they are gone. Never seen again."

"My father once told me, no one ever really gets rid of a useful weapon. They may put it away, but they always know where it is." Hopwell was grim, his face dark. "Chastisers were and, by my guess, still are a useful weapon."

"You're just grasping at straws." Layten didn't even want to think about it. He had never grown up particularly religious though. He followed Sartum of course and hated magic like a good northerner. But the idea of the Chastisers still being around was not one he liked at all.

"Maybe. But just so we are all protected, we must make a promise. Right here, and right now. Anything we read here we only discuss here. Not in our room. Not in public. Not to anyone else." Hopwell raised his head and looked at the guardian again and gave a small shudder. "I do not plan on even setting foot in this place again. I'd rather be safe and alive."

Layten saw that appeal, he did, but he also felt something else. His eyes fell again to the leather tome, tied with a blue cord. Knowledge. Truth. It was the whole reason he'd wanted to be a Scholar. Well, that and not spending the rest of his life making paper on the edge of a marsh in the backwater of Lowter.

"What do you say, Layten?" Wix asked. "I had not thought about the things that could happen. Maybe I should have not shown you all this. Maybe not have come here."

"I…" Layten shrugged. "I do not know." But he did know. He wondered why he had lied. He would be back here. And soon. Even if it was alone. He had to know. He had to.

"Let us get back to our room, get cleaned up. It will be time to eat soon." Hopwell pushed them towards the ruined corner. "And I don't want to miss the excitement of watching Layten turn as red as Delerie's hair as he tries to be clever and charming."

"I said shut it!" Layten snapped again, but with a laugh, diffusing the tension and sense of dread that had started to clench at his heart. Wix led the way, this time followed by Hopwell as they squeezed through the crack, leaving Layten alone.

"Soon," he whispered, his eyes on the books.

"Get stuck again, Layten?" Hop asked from the other side of the wall. "Come on, this little… excursion has taken too long already."

"Coming... coming..." Layten grumbled and squeezed his way back through the break into the stone hallway. The walk back was quiet, each of them thinking about what they had seen. And Layten memorized every twist, every turn, and every door to find his way back.

"Did they listen?" Binin asked as she slumped down in her favorite chair in Fean's office. "Let me guess. The lords ignored you, and the priests thumbed their noses at you and said you weren't sufficiently humble."

"Not exactly." Fean closed his eyes and forced himself to relax. Some days the gibbering madness that nearly filled him came close to being revealed. Today had been one of those days.

"Well then?" Wilk was also in his customary spot, by the lone window, overlooking the largest courtyard of the Anchorhold.

"They listened." Fean shrugged. "Most seemed to already know about danger. Or at least heard about it through rumors. The Lords were more receptive to the idea of more Anchor patrols. Though some of the more rural nobles were clearly uncomfortable with the idea."

"Would they rather deal with the things themselves? They can play with mistsnakes and turnknots themselves." Binin shook her head. "I know. I shouldn't expect any more respect."

"They are just scared. They see the increase in the sightings. They expect the Anchors to keep them safe as we have for generations. They don't see the problems though, the way villagers hide when an Anchor is spotted, so they can't tell us anything of what they have seen." Fean poured himself a glass of vitae and took a long drink. "They respect us but are terrified of us all at the same time."

"That doesn't help anyone." Wilk crossed his arms. "The Priests?"

"As usual, they were…more zealous. I had them though… until the question got asked. The question I feared." Fean took another sip. "How many Anchors are there? It was from that Priest from Hattersand."

"The young one?" Binin frowned. "Isn't he the one who wanted to question the loyalty of all the Anchors? Make them all 'prove' their love of Sartum? And outlaw the Protector order?"

"One and the same." Fean shook his head. "He's got delusions that the Priesthood should get rid of the Anchors and take care of any issues themselves."

"They can't," Wilk snorted. "But they don't know that."

"Exactly. Only the Elder Anchors know. And their Protectors." Fean watched a single drop of moisture roll down the side of the metal tumbler, clinging to the zig-zag pattern and moving with it, gathering more moisture before the weight of it all made the whole thing fall on to his desk. A fitting sight for a day like this.

"I had to tell them then. About the losses. For a time, I thought I'd escaped without having to talk about it." Fean shrugged. "They did not take it well. The Lords started yelling. The Priests started pointing fingers. Not all of them of course. Some looked sorrowful. But the same idiots as normal."

"And now what?" Wilk asked. "Will it come to war?"

"I do not know." Fean drank the last drop of vitae, wishing he could get drunk. "They kicked me out and started yelling again at each other. Not in anger, but to see who would control the meeting. So, we will wait... wait and see. I doubt anyone will decide anything today. Messengers will have to be sent; questions answered. But…." Fean rubbed his head with both hands. "I just don't know."

Chapter Twenty-Four

Layten yawned, half sitting up in his bed, and winced, as the spot that Hop had struck was still sore. He was pretty sure he had a bruise from that strike. It had been a very strange night after they had gotten back to their room. None of them had felt like talking much. They had gotten cleaned up, and eaten, and both Wix and Hop had vanished with women out into the House. Wix with Luiy, and Hop… well... who knew with Hop. Neither had come back last night either. Layten slumped back down and tried to remember exactly how to get back to that place Wix had found. He was almost sure he could get back there without too much trouble. Almost.

All the Apprentices had heard the stories about students who wandered out into the maze that the House of Knowledge was and vanished. Never to be seen again. Or, maybe worse, stumble out, old and gray-haired. One rumor said the Scholars had a special team that would go out at the end of the year and gather and dispose of all the students who had vanished that year. Their corpses at least.

The obvious flaw with that nonsense was that no one ever saw anyone vanish. Just 'rumors' of someone vanishing. Apprentices said it was Journeymen, and Journeymen said it was Apprentices. Scholars said nothing but rolled their eyes if they were asked.

It was true that the House was far larger than it had any right to be. They actually only took up a tiny part of the place. Layten had read that all the Houses were far larger inside than they needed to be, for reasons known only to Sartum.

The door burst open, and Hopwell walked in grinning. "Good morning, Layten! Sleeping alone again last night?"

"In fact, Delerie just left," Layten answered back. It wasn't true of course. They had talked some last night, but his quiet mood and introspective bent had clashed with her annoyance at him still not getting the hint. They had parted with a nod instead of a hug at least.

"Oh really?" Hopwell sat on his bed. "Do tell."

Layten shook his head. "You know I'm just kidding, Hop."

"And that, my good friend, is why you could never be a noble. A good noble always knows how to lie."

Hopwell threw himself down on the bed with a smile. "I for one had a wonderful evening with a certain exotic beauty."

Layten knew he had to mean Tildeim. She was from a small island just off the southeastern coast. Blood Moon Bay was her backyard. Layten liked Tildeim. She was smart and funny. And she did not suffer fools, which, when it came to Hop, made him wonder. "How do I know you're telling the truth?" Layten pointed out. "You just said nobles know how to lie."

"Good catch." Hopwell sighed. "You don't know. You will never know. But you also won't ask Tildeim."

"Why wouldn't I?" Layten sat all the way up now. "I mean, she's just down the hall."

"Because Layten, you're too shy to do so." Hopwell sat back up as well. "One day you're going to have to realize that that shyness is keeping you from the truth of a lot of things. You don't ask because you are scared to know."

The door opened then, cutting off Layten's retort. Wix. The little man was disheveled, more so than usual. "Hello good friends."

"Have a good night with Luiy?" Hop asked with a grin. "I was just pointing out to Layten here that his shyness and unwillingness to ask about certain topics will always come back to hurt him."

"Yes, good night." Wix smiled, but something was off. It seemed somewhat forced, like he was playing the part of Wix, but really didn't want to.

"You feeling well?" Hop asked as Wix crawled into his bed and lay still.

"Fine. I feel fine." Wix rolled over. "I went back."

"Oh." Layten and Hop exchanged looks. They weren't supposed to talk about it, but it was obvious something was bothering their friend. "Did Luiy…"

"No, she went back to her room long time ago. I was up all night. Reading, studying." Wix rubbed his head. "Hungry and tired. That is all. Hungry and tired."

"Good thing it's restday then." Hop yawned himself. "I'm not exactly well-rested myself. See Layten, there's the upside to your situation. You get plenty of sleep."

"Ha," Layten threw back at him. "Well then, am I going to eat alone?"

Wix didn't answer, and Layten could see he was already asleep. Hopwell lay back down. "For now, yes. I'll see you later… lunchtime. Unless Tildiem comes looking for me of course."

Layten didn't answer. If he had, Hopwell wouldn't stop his comments. He was right in one way though. Layten had to deal with this shyness that gripped him in some situations. Especially those situations involving Delerie Kilmeed. He'd made friends quick enough, why was expressing interest so hard?

Because she was an attractive, fun, interesting woman, that was why. A woman who would be looking for him at breakfast, unless she'd gotten bored of him. A possibility that made him feel even worse about the whole thing if that was possible. He got ready quietly, as by the time he left the washroom, both Hopwell and Wix were asleep.

Layten started to leave and then, in a pinch grabbed a writing rod, and the half-empty white book he had gotten back in Giller. He'd not had a chance to really do much with it, or even read most of it. With it being restday he didn't have anything assigned, or any classes to go to.

A number of students would be out in town; the Inkwell Inn, the Scroll and Feather, and a few other places would be crawling with people this afternoon, and this evening. A mix of students and townspeople. Not a few young rich merchants' sons either, intent on loving and leaving a student or two. There had already been one fight apparently, at least the rumor had it.

A very well-off towner, as they were apparently called, had attempted to make some time with a female student, though who exactly was not known. Another student had stepped in after the said student told the towner to go away. Fists had been thrown, and a few chairs.

Everyone had run away when the city guard had shown up though. And there were so many versions of the story no one really knew who was at fault. Apparently, the towner had refused to talk as he'd been hit with a chair so hard, he'd been knocked unconscious.

Layten had thought after that sort of nonsense people would go less, he'd only gone twice, and both times found it too noisy and too expensive. He still didn't like crowds that much. Give him the silence or quiet sounds of the forest, or a library. A crowded, noisy inn? No, thank you. But the rumors just made most people go more often.

Hopwell went all the time. He'd be at the Ink Well tonight, Layten was sure of it. It seemed the students sort of split into two groups, ones who liked the Ink Well and those who preferred the Scroll and Feather. Layten couldn't tell any difference in the places, but Hopwell insisted the Ink Well was better. He'd invite Wix and Layten, he always did.

Wix would go only if Luiy wanted to. Layten just begged off. Hop never stopped trying to get Layten to go, something that Layten liked for some odd reason. A splash of red in sunlight brought his attention back to here and now. Delerie.

She was talking to another student. A male student. And laughing. And her hand was on his arm, giving it a squeeze. For Layten it seemed his whole world slowed and almost stopped. Who was that? What were they talking about? Why was she... touching him?

The other student laughed, and Layten got a glimpse of his face. Ottor. Ottor Windviel. That did not make Layten feel any better. Ottor was a Journeyman firstly. He was an assistant for Scholar Qualtin, who taught geography. Layten didn't have that class yet; he'd have it next year. Ottor however had almost the same reputation as Hopwell did.

Handsome, funny, smart… Ottor had more than his fair share. He was known also to take 'interest' in apprentices. The kind of interest that made Layten very unhappy. His stomach fell even more when he saw Ottor offer her his arm, and they walked off together. He started to go after them. He took a dozen steps, determined to... Layten stopped. Do what? Delerie had gotten sick of waiting for him to do something. He'd gotten in his own way too many times, and she'd lost interest. There was nothing for him to do. He could imagine himself storming after them, professing his true feelings and her gracefully accepting them. Imagine. But this wasn't some fluff romantic play. He'd hesitated too much, and he'd lost his chance. And it had only been a chance. She might have realized that he was, in truth, rather boring. He didn't like to go out. He liked the quiet. He was nondescript. He wasn't ugly, but neither was he terribly good-looking. The more he considered it, the more he realized she was better off without him.

He also wasn't hungry now. And the thought of seeing her with Ottor… well, he'd rather skip a few meals. Layten glanced down at his hand, still holding the marking rod and the journal. That place Wix showed him. That was the place to go. No one but Hopwell and Wix would come there, and they were both asleep. He had no desire to see anyone or talk to anyone right now. Layten turned and walked away, trying very hard to not think about anything else than where he was going.

He was somewhat surprised he found his way back without too much effort. He pushed the wall just so, like Wix had done, and the wall slid away, showing the same door. The orb almost at once made him feel empty and cold. It was worse now though. For a long moment he wondered if he'd ever be happy again. A gnawing icy grip on his mind grew. His stomach churned, and he almost felt like if he took a single step he'd fall. Fall into a dark and empty void that he'd never escape from.

Would that be so bad? No pain. No hurt. No sorrow. A whispering voice echoed in his mind. A voice that mixed with agonized screams of horror and torment. *You are close. I can help you join with us. Just ask, and you can be free of this hurt. Forever.* Layten blinked and shuddered, and the voice faded away.

"Just my imagination. I've always hated those things," Layten muttered, finding his way to the crack again. This time he managed to get in without tearing anything, but he did knock a small piece of old masonry off where it had been perched, and it fell to the floor with an echoing clatter.

The sound seemed so much louder in this place. Loud enough that Layten faced the guardian here, hoping that if it did move, he'd be able to get back into the hallway in time. But the sound did nothing to the machine, and it sat there, the same slumped-over broken look it seemed to always have.

Putting his things down, Layten approached the book he'd seen the last time. The leather-bound book, tied with a bright blue cord. The blue called to him for some reason. He couldn't take his eyes off it, at least not without effort. He tore his eyes away long enough to check the guardian. Unmoving. His hands trembled, and suddenly felt sweaty as he moved them closer to the book.

He paused. Sweat could damage this, couldn't it? He wiped them several times on his robes, managing to get them mostly dry. He reached towards the book again, his whole body giving a tremor as he touched the cover. The book was cold to the touch. Cold, yet, soft. He slowly untied the blue cord, giving another glance towards the danger that slumbered by the door.

It sat still, as Wix had said. Just don't take it too far from the floating table it was on, and it should be fine. Right? That was what he'd said. The cord pulled free, lying on the table. Layten opened the book slowly. The pages were old, thin. And he began to read.

Chapter Twenty-Five

I, Jinir, former Tarn of the City in Blue, write this in hopes that maybe one day, someone will understand. I am far too ensnared now in the trap set by Sartum to ever escape. A trap I put myself in, A trap made of my own cowardice. I should have died in the City. I should have faced death and fought. But I ran. I ran and hid. And I lived because of it. If this is life. I now work to further the aims of a god I do not believe in, a god I do not follow. A god, that... is wrong.

I find a tiny piece of solace in the fact that the god does not even know what his name means. Sartum. Myriam VolFar named him. The fact that it's the name for donkey droppings does bring a slight smile to my face, even now. I should have done more to help her. I should have helped Rauger, and not let my fears cloud my judgment. And Ralta... I knew you loved me. You loved me, and I used that fact. Forgive me, my Trinil friend. I failed you most of all.

Layten stopped reading, his thoughts a jumble. This was a journal? Belonging to High Prophet Jinir? The man who switched sides at the War of Betrayal and joined the side of good? But this was all wrong. This sounded like he... he didn't like it. He wasn't a true believer. And donkey droppings? That was heresy. Wrong!

Layten stepped back from the book, fighting the urge to throw it across the room. A fake. Yes, it had to be a fake. It must be a fake. A trap for those who came here. A trap to do what? Make someone doubt the truth. But why? Layten swallowed, his mouth dry. He couldn't think of a reason. And if there wasn't one, then...maybe it wasn't a lie.

Layten fumbled for the white journal he'd brought and his marking rod. He was thankful he'd filled it last night, bored and wondering if he should go find Delerie. An involuntary snort escaped him. That would have been a better use of his time. But that was gone now.

He had to take notes. He had to see if he could corroborate any of the things he had just read. If he could, in some small way, then maybe he'd read more. Maybe. "Sartum guide me," Layten whispered to himself and then stopped. His mind filled with the image of donkey droppings. "That's going to stick with me for a long time. Thanks, book," he whispered again. He wrote a single word. 'Donkey' and closed it. If he could find ANYTHING like that in the more normal rooms... he'd... well he'd come back. The idea terrified him. Or was that excitement? His feelings were jumbled up. He might have found a horrible secret that fascinated him all the same. He had to leave. Yes, get some space, time to think.

What had his father said once? 'What you think is what you are.' Or something like that. If that was true, he must be quite the sight, since right now, he didn't know what to think. He looked at the book, wondering if he should tie it back up. If he left it like that, it would be obvious someone had read it. But the only people who came here were Wix, Hopwell, and himself. And Hop said he'd never come back.

And would Wix care? No, he doubted he would. But yet, leaving it like that seemed disrespectful. So slowly, he closed the book and retied the blue cord as best he could. There was also the question of whether the Guardian would react if he left the book not as he'd found it. Just to be safe then, right?

Layten exited again through the crack, finding it easier now. One, he'd not eaten anything, and his stomach was empty. Food right now didn't seem all that appealing, too much else on his mind. And that small piece of stone and masonry had been the one that had scraped his back last time, he was sure of it.

He exited, brushing dust off his robes and fast walking past the door with the orb, the sound of the screams somewhat muted by his own inner turmoil. Something he was a little grateful for. He closed the stone hallway off again and began the walk back to the more usual parts of the House of Knowledge.

"Apprentice Grayread, we meet again." A thin shape walked out of a dim section of the hallway that Layten was in. Master Retuin.

Layten was surprised by this fact. He'd kind of forgotten about the ink maker in the day-to-day of the school. The Trinil was dressed in a kind of form-fitting red and green outfit. Certainly nothing like the robes Scholars wore.

"Master Retuin!" Layten lowered his head in respect. "My apologies Master, I did not mean to disturb you." Layten tried to bypass the ink maker and continue on his way.

"Oh, I was looking for you. You did not disturb me." Master Retuin gave him a curious look again, and Layten could not help but remember that first night here. "I am in fact in need of your help."

"My help?" Layten didn't know what to say. "Sorry, Master Retuin."

"Yes, your help. I need something special. A special kind of paper. I was hoping you could reach out to your father and give my request to him." Master Retuin smiled. It was just too large.

Layten did not like his smile. It felt forced, like he'd practiced it in a mirror to get it right but failed. "Oh. I guess." His hands unclenched some. Passing on a paper request from the Ink primary wouldn't be too hard a stretch. Nothing to worry about.

"Excellent. Excellent." Master Retuin pulled a thin folded parchment out, one sealed with green wax. "Can you send this with a personal request from you? See, I have attempted to get this request to him before. Half a dozen times. But I have yet to ever receive a reply. So, I am assuming he's not reading them."

"He always reads requests!" Layten's voice rose before he remembered who he was talking to. "I'm sorry, Master Retuin. I'll bet he never got the requests. Mail is a slow thing to Lowter. I wrote them early on to let them know I was here, and it took a full month to get a reply."

"Ah, yes." Retuin lowered his head. "Very true. Well, if you are willing to try, here is the letter with my request."

Layten took the parchment, feeling a slick oiliness from it that he didn't recognize. Must be from an animal skin. "I will, Master."

"What, if I may ask, are you doing in this section of the House? No one ever comes this way. It's the reason my laboratory and quarters are here." Master Retuin pointed to a door that was half hidden in the dim lighting.

"Just was looking for some quiet." Layten scrambled to come up with something to add. "Bad morning."

"Ah. Say no more. The tribulations of the apprentice heart." Master Retuin smiled again; a smile that once more seemed forced, almost practiced. "I thank you for your assistance."

"You are welcome…" Layten started to say but the Trinil Ink primary had already turned and walked away. Not towards his labs and quarters but in a direction that Layten had not explored. His long legs carried him quickly out of view.

Layten examined the parchment he'd been given, the oily feel of it was strong. Almost slick. What kind of ink could even soak into parchment like this? Layten knew paper. He'd never seen paper like this one. Paper needed to be clean, and absorbent enough that ink would soak in the top layers, but not all the way through. There was a method to making it work. This… letter, was far too thin and far too oily. And holding it up to what light there was made him even more confused. He could see through it. And there was nothing written on it. Not a single mark that would show writing could he see.

He was tempted to break the seal and examine it further. The whole encounter had bothered him, and this lasting reminder of it made little sense. But he had said he would mail this to his father. He'd given assurances.

Placing the paper in his book, he continued on his way, heading back to his room, his thoughts a jumble.

Fean threw down the scroll he'd been given. Fools. And to make it worse, that Priest... Vilom, the one from Hattersand, had managed to push through something even worse. A new position, and of course, he'd been named to the role. 'Voice of Sartum' indeed. What it meant was nothing good. Now, all reports and information that the Anchors had must be turned over to this new leader in the faith. Every scrap.

Even worse, if he was reading this correctly, it should go to this new leader before it went to anyone else. And then the Voice of Sartum would decide who got it, if anyone. All in the name of keeping the peace. Peace. Fean could see where this would go.

There had always been a faction in the Priesthood who were on the lookout for an excuse for a more forceful response to magic from the south. They alternatively accused the Anchors of not rooting it out more, and at the same time preached that the Anchors were tainted by their work. And now, having one of their own in a single seat controlling who got to see what?

They wanted a war. A wholesale invasion of the south. They wanted to remake Sartum's glorious victory and the City in Blue, without the betrayal by the hated ones, William Reis and Myriam VolFar. As if the war would solve anything. Magic would still exist. There would just be a lot fewer people around to either use it or fight it.

Fean poured himself a cup of water, even though he really wanted something stronger, and gulped it down. He had to think of a way to get past this. He was the Navigator of the Anchorhold, after all.

Chapter Twenty-Six

"Layten!" Hopwell was sitting up, and actually doing work for class when Layten returned to the room, finally. "Breakfast must have gone well; you've been gone half the day."

"No, it did not." Layten shook his head. "Trust me, this has not been a good day at all."

"What?" Wix raised a head out of his bed. "Share." Layten sat on his own bed, trying to come up with a good way to explain everything that had happened. "Well, Delerie is now with Ottor, that Journeyman? I went to a very quiet place and read something that… I didn't like. And on top of it, on the way back I had a very odd encounter with that Trinil, Master Retuin."

Hopwell put his work down, his expression grim. "Right. Let's talk this through then. Wix?"

Wix nodded and sat up. "Go Layten, explain."

Layten grimaced. He had no desire to go through all that again, but they were his friends, and he knew they wanted to help, or at least make him feel better. "I was on my way to breakfast and saw them... together. I guess you were right Hop, I waited too long. I don't blame her. She waited around for me to do... something, and I didn't.

"Then, I well... I didn't want to go to breakfast obviously. So, I decided to go to that quiet spot Wix showed us. Someplace I could be alone. And I read something. Something I need to investigate. Something wrong." Layten pulled out the paper the ink primary had given him. "And then, I run into Master Retuin. He gives me this and asks me to mail it to my father. Says it's a special request. But, it's blank. And the paper feels strange. Oily."

Wix's face had moved from expressionless to frowning as Layten had spoken. "Ottor. I do not like that man. Good looking men are usually bad."

"What?" Hopwell gave an exclamation of fake horror.

"You may be an exception. I will decide later," Wix smirked. "But this is about Layten."

"True." Hop frowned. "Ottor is a problem we may be able to fix. He's got quite the reputation. Even more than I do."

"There is nothing to fix." Layten shook his head. "I appreciate it. I really do. But the facts are simple. I waited too long. And who knows, it's not as if she were promised to me. She may have decided rather quickly that I wasn't exactly anything she wanted to spend time with."

"Hush." Wix waved a hand. "You are a good man. And not too good looking."

"Thanks, maybe," Layten smirked. "Delerie has every right to do whatever she wants. My feelings are hurt of course, but it wasn't like I didn't have my chances. Chances I did not take. Chances that Hop here kept telling me about."

"See, I AM a good man, Wix." Hop shook a finger at Wix. "And you are right. But I am sorry." Hop paused. "What did you read?"

"Something I don't like," Layten shrugged. "I need to try and research some ideas. If anything bears fruit, I'll let you know."

Wix, Hop, and Layten all exchanged glances, and nodded. Their agreement still stood. None of that was to be discussed in detail here. "So, you met the mystery Trinil again?" Hop changed the subject to the final issue. "I wish I'd been there with you. I don't think anyone has seen him but you, at least among the apprentices."

"Yes. This strikes me as very strange." Wix got off his bed and paced. "A Trinil who should not be here. And you, and just you, interact with him twice. You say he was looking for you?"

"Yes. But he wanted me to send this letter that appears just to be parchment for him. Maybe he sealed the wrong parchment and got them mixed up or something." Layten waved the letter again. "That might explain why it feels so slick and odd."

"I see where Wix is going with this. Think, Layten. He was looking for you, in that location. Why would he look there?" Hopwell twirled his marking rod between his fingers in thought. "Did he say anything else?"

"No, he did say his lab and living quarters were there and pointed to a room." Layten shrugged. "The only odd thing, well… things, was the fact that after giving me the parchment, he walked away, but not towards most of the House, or back to his lab. He went some other way, and fast."

"What was the other strange thing?" Wix had stopped pacing and was looking at the parchment, as if his very sight could make it readable.

"His smile. It just felt… off. Fake. Like he'd practiced it in a mirror as if to say, 'I can smile.' But it didn't look like he wanted to smile." Layten frowned. "If that makes sense. It's probably in my head. I don't know any Trinil. Maybe they all smile that way."

"Maybe. Maybe not." Hopwell frowned. "We should open it."

"What, the letter?" Layten held the paper up. "I thought about it, but I promised to send it to my father."

"Did you promise not to open it?" Wix grinned. "I know how to open that and seal it back up without being discovered."

Layten looked at the parchment. He was curious, and it all seemed too strange. He'd not thought about what Hop had asked. It didn't make sense for Retuin to be right there, waiting for him. No one knew he was there. It could have been blind luck. He'd just come out of his lab and seen Layten; strange things can happen sometimes.
But he still felt bad about opening it. He'd not EXACTLY said he'd not open it. But he'd certainly given that impression. "I don't know. I didn't say I wouldn't open it, but…"
Wix shrugged. "We could see if that is really his lab. Then we would know if he was really waiting for you."
"That my friend, is an excellent idea." Hopwell stood up. "After lunch of course."
"Lunch." Layten was hungry, but the idea of seeing Delerie and Ottor together… was going to happen regardless of what he did. He needed to stop moping about it. It's not like they were ever together anyway.
"You are right. I'm hungry."
"That's the idea," Hop grinned. "Well, let's get cleaned up, Wix."
"Yes, fine. I am hungry as well." Wix smiled. "We shall get this all taken care of today. Maybe go… someplace quiet as well."
"Maybe," Hopwell frowned. "We will see."
"Thanks," Layten mumbled. He was grateful for his friends.
"No need to thank us. We have not done anything yet." Wix grinned. "Yet."

It was a short time later when both Wix and Hopwell
were ready to go. There was already a somewhat steady
stream of students heading towards the dining area.
Luiy approached Wix, but Wix whispered something to
her, and she shot a look at Layten and nodded, and
returned to her roommate's side.

"You can go with her, it's fine," Layten said as Wix
rejoined them.

"No. You have need of a friend. I am one of them."
Wix slapped Layten on the back.

They found their customary table quickly and found a
nice enough lunch of roasted fowl, mushrooms, brown
bread with butter, and some kind of bean that Layten
didn't know. After not having breakfast, it all was
delicious to him. He also kept his eyes on his friends,
and not on the redhead two tables away. He also tried
very hard not to pay attention to her laugh.

"Don't worry, Layten. It will all work out." Hopwell
kept his voice low. "Besides, I have an idea I wanted to
talk to you both about."

"Oh? This should be good." Layten sat back, grateful to
have something else to keep him busy.

"You know how my father has a Scholar? Remember
that? When Kof made a big fuss over it?" Hop pushed
his food around on his plate, looking
uncharacteristically unsure of himself.

"Yes. Though mostly that was because he was annoyed
with you spilling ink everywhere," Layten pointed out.

"Yes, well… I've been thinking. When I take over as
Golmor, I'll need a new Scholar. And… I was hoping,
Layten, you might be willing to think about the role. I
would need someone I trust. Someone who will tell me
the truth." Hopwell raised his eyes to meet Layten's.
"What do you think?"

Layten was surprised, he'd not given any real thought to what he would do after he was a full Scholar. Being offered the spot of Scholar for Hopwell was a very generous offer. A noble's scholar was a high-ranking member of that noble's court. Guaranteed a nice place to live, a good salary, and more. "I don't know what to say."

"Oh, I see, leave Wix out." Wix smiled. "You did not tell him you offered it to me already and I turned you down."

"What?" Layten for some reason felt his face turn red. Wix smirked for a moment and then broke into laughter pointing at the faces of both Layten and Hopwell who were both giving him shocked expressions. "Ah! You are both so easy to surprise. I joke of course. But Hopwell, I am not someone you trust? You know how to hurt a man's feelings."

Hopwell broke into a laugh of his own. "Wix, I trust you. But I have a different idea for you. But we will discuss that another time."

"Now I am curious, young noble. You are almost becoming the first noble I truly like." Wix speared a bean. "I do not like beans. But I will eat it anyway." And did so, with a slight grimace.

"Well?" Hopwell asked again. "What do you think, Layten?"

"Yes." Layten felt better as soon as he said it. "I thank you. But remember, I'll tell you when you are being an ass, or when you are wrong."

"That is exactly why you are the right choice." Hopwell stood suddenly. "Now it wouldn't be for a few years. I must finish my rounding, and you have to finish here." Hop looked down at his plate. "I'm done."

Layten nodded. "I know." He stood as well and, giving a smirk, bowed to Hopwell. "My Golmor."

Hop rolled his eyes. "Wonderful."

"Yes, let us go. I am curious." Wix stood too. "And don't pay attention, but Delerie has been watching you for half the lunch with a very sad expression on her face."

Layten didn't answer but felt a small sense of satisfaction that he at once hated himself for. "Well, let's… go." Hopwell led the way, purposefully walking the long way around, avoiding any chance encounters for Layten.

Chapter Twenty- Seven

"Well Layten, lead the way." Hop had stopped around the corner. "I'm curious to see this Trinil, if he's still about."

"You say that like you don't believe me," Layten scoffed. "He's real."

"Oh, I believe you. But him being here still doesn't make sense." Hop frowned. "Remember, all she said was the Trinil being here was the Church of Sartum approved. Which presents its own issues."

"The Church of Sartum is a very mixed place," Wix added. "Back in Ture there are very good and kind people who are part of the church. And there are people who would enjoy peeling the skin off your body for something to do."

"What a pleasant picture," Hopwell added. "Either way, I think we would all prefer to NOT be on the bad side of the church, or Sartum himself."

"To that I think we all agree." Layten did not even want to entertain the idea. "Follow me."

Layten led his friends deeper into the House. Remembering the turns and doors he'd taken before. "I still do not understand how this place can be this big. And why it's this big is even more of a mystery."

"It's not a mystery." Wix shrugged. "If you can think like a god."

"What do you mean?" Hopwell added an edge of noble condescension to his question.

"It's simple. There are fixed places in the house. The rest forms around you as needed." Wix shrugged. "I do not think this place is really even in Timik."

The idea of the House of Knowledge not really being in Timik and forming around them as needed made Layten's head hurt. He had no idea where Wix had come up with this idea, but he certainly did not like it. His revulsion at magic had abated a fair amount since he'd been here, if just because hints of the force were around them all the time. But the idea that everything they were seeing was... somehow built by magic as needed, did nothing to help his disgust.

Hopwell made a grimace, but did not answer Wix's statement about the whole place. Layten was pretty sure he did not like the idea either. Who could like it? It all made him uneasy. Thankfully, he entered a hallway that looked like the others, but had a wooden door, plain, set in the shadows. "This is the place. That door."

"Good." Hopwell strode over to the door, giving the impression he might just kick it down, but paused. "Soo... do I just knock first?"

"You don't have a plan?" Layten asked, looking around. "I thought you had a plan."

"Well, I was working on one, then Wix brought up the building forming around us and then all I could think of was the place deciding not to and leaving us... someplace else." Hopwell scowled. "I... I have a fear of falling. I got distracted."

Layten knew right then that Hopwell considered them true friends. There was no way the proud young noble would tell anyone he didn't trust that piece of information. He could have been lying, sure, but his words rung true. He and Wix locked eyes for a second and nodded. They would keep that secret.

"Yes. Knock first. And then if he doesn't answer. I will... get us in." Wix smiled. "I was not always this charming and amusing apprentice scholar, you know."

"You aren't a charming and amusing scholar now," Hopwell retorted but took a large breath and let it out. "Fine." His hand hovered over the door for a moment and then, gave it four hard knocks.

Silence followed the knocks. Layten realized he was holding his breath and let it out, earning a glance from Hopwell. "Sorry," Layten whispered.

Hopwell knocked again, four hard knocks. The sound echoed down the hall, and Layten half expected master Retuin to come striding down the hall, annoyed at the noise. But silence again was the only answer. It almost seemed more silent, if that was a possibility.

"Well. I do not think he is home." Wix reached into his robe pocket and pulled out a tiny bundle. "Keep watch."

"What is that?" Layten was confused.

"Lockpicks? Are you a thief, Wix?" Hopwell had that disapproving noble tone in his voice again.

"You learn things. Pick a lock or starve, which do you do?" Wix shrugged, he did not appear to be bothered by Hopwell's disapproval. A disapproval that vanished quickly and a grin broke out.

"Nice skill to have."

That, for some reason, gave Wix pause. "You are a very strange noble, Hopwell Lewin."

Hop stepped back from the door, allowing Wix access to the door lock. Whatever he did was over quickly as there was a noticeable click sound and Wix stepped back. "There. Old lock. Easy."

"Did you know he could do that?" Hop leaned over to Layten, his voice low.

"No idea." Layten wasn't surprised, at least, not exactly. Wix had been open with the fact that he'd grown up poor and on the streets of Ture. The fact that he might pick up some more 'morally ambiguous' skills made sense.

"Well, are you going to open it?' Hop asked standing next to Layten still.

"No. I leave that to you. If there is someone in there, it is better they see you, Hopwell. You are a noble, and not a regular student. They would be much harsher on Layten, or I." Wix walked away from the door, stopping only when he was slightly behind Layten.

"You make a good shield Layten." Wix grinned. "Open the door Hopwell."

"Fine." Hop sighed and approached the door once more. He gave it one more set of four knocks, and then, without much of a wait, pushed the door open.

Layten couldn't see anything from where he was. "Well?"

"Our Trinil friend was lying." Hop pushed the door all the way open, to show them both what was inside. The room was empty. Totally completely empty. At least this room was. A thin layer of dust covered the room, lying on worktables and a few wooden chairs. There was another door on the far wall that was closed, so who knew what was in that room.

"Maybe." Wix walked into the room, followed by both Layten and Hopwell. "Look. The wood is stained."

"He's right." Layten examined several of the workbenches. All of them had various stains on them, usually dark blue or black ones. But a splash of color existed a few places. There were also scorch marks, including a rather badly burned corner of one table. "This may have been used to make ink, in the past."

"Past. But not anytime recently." Hopwell dragged a finger through the dust. "This wasn't laid in a day or a month."

"True." Layten approached the far door. This one didn't appear to have a lock, just a simple handle. He took a breath and pulled it open. Only to be disappointed again. It was empty as well, but had, just like the first room, been used at some point in the past. It had been a bedroom. A plain bed, though larger than theirs stood in the middle of the room. The furniture was nicer but still fairly plain. But the same layer of dust overlayed everything.

"Why so much dust? We barely see any in the rest of the place." Layten coughed; the dust was worse in this room than the last.

"Who knows?" Wix shrugged. "I do not think it is important though. But what this does show us is that this Master Retuin was lying to you. Which means we need to open that letter."

"I agree with Wix. This is all too convenient." Hopwell frowned. "I don't like it."

Layten had agreed to come here and do this hoping that this would be the lab and quarters of the Trinil. But now that they knew it wasn't, or at least, wasn't currently, he found himself backed into a corner. *I didn't say I wouldn't open it. But I don't want to feel like I lied.* Layten frowned. *But he lied to me, so...*

"Fine. Back at the room we will open it." Layten turned towards his friends. "But for now, let's go someplace quiet."

Both Wix and Hopwell knew what he meant, but their reactions were different. Wix grinned, and for some reason rubbed his hands together, excited. Hop looked almost dejected by the idea. Layten knew that he hadn't wanted to go back there, and half expected Hopwell to leave them here and head back to their rooms.

"Fine," Hopwell shrugged, and motioned for them to move onward.

Back out in the hallway, Wix looked around. "Which way did this mysterious Trinil go when you saw him leave?"

Layten stopped to think, so many of these hallways and twists looked exactly the same, sometimes It was hard to make sense of it. "I think it was that way, he took that turn. I didn't hear any doors, but I also didn't stay around, I left."

"Noted for later exploration," Wix nodded and started towards the mysterious room.

"How did you find this place exactly?" Layten asked. "I'm still not clear."

"I like exploring. Back home I often explored older parts of Ture. Even the sewers." Wix smiled. "The sewers of Ture are old, very old. Not like most places."

"Sewers??" Hopwell grimaced. "The smell alone would drive me away."

"Smell? Yes, not good. But no worse than some of the slums in Ture. I have heard once that years ago, Ture had no slums. Even in the poorest parts of the city, they kept the houses up. The city did. But that was long ago. Now, there are slums." Wix frowned.

"But I like to explore. And it's safer here than outside the House." Wix pushed the stone wall, the secret opening sliding open with the barest of grinding noises. "And you were looking for a place to take Luiy," Hopwell added.

"Yes. Her roommate snores." Wix shrugged. "She is a nice girl. I like her very much."

Layten knew the moment the door was finished opening, even if he hadn't been watching. The orb. The thing sat there, shiny black, and the now familiar feeling of ice cold and emptiness filled him. He didn't hear a voice talking, at least not now. The scream was there though, barely able to be heard. He hated the screaming.

"Layten?" Hop poked him.

"What?" Layten blinked, shifting his eyes away from the orb, and its gnawing hunger.

"You just stood there for a while. Staring at that thing in the door. You want to leave?" Hopwell almost sounded happy at the idea.

"No, sorry. Just in thought," Layten grinned, mostly to set Hop at ease. He was glad he didn't hear that voice this time. It had to have been his imagination. He was so confused when he had left. That was it. Just confusion, lack of food, and just not in the right mind. The crack was there, and getting through it was still tight, but doable. Everything seemed the exact same. Wix was already in the room, and Hopwell followed him into the place. "Ok, now talk. What bothered you so much?" Hopwell asked keeping his face towards Layten.

"This book. It appears to be a journal, from High Prophet Jinir. It... it says things."

Chapter Twenty-Eight

"Of course, it says things. It's a book." Hop grinned. "What kind of things?"

"That he regretted it. That he never believed in Sartum. That Sartum's name…." Layten looked down. "That his name, from Myriam VolFar, meant... donkey droppings."

Wix suppressed a laugh. "True? That would mean a lot to certain people I know."

"That's sacrilege." Hopwell dropped his smile and scowled at the book. "It must be a fake."

"Why? Because it says things you don't like?" Wix argued back. "Think Hopwell. Myriam VolFar, one of the pair who made and named the reborn god. She did not like him, correct? So, she named him that as a bit of revenge." Wix grinned. "Well played, long gone woman."

"No, it's NOT well played. She is one of the betrayers! Her and that William Reis. Villains both of them." Hopwell shook his head. "Do not even think of ever saying that to anyone else, either of you. Do you know what the Priesthood would do if they ever found out about that book?"

"Burn it." Wix shrugged. "It's what they do."

"Or a lot worse. I told you, Layten, there are groups within the Priesthood. If they make someone vanish for even using Sartum's name in a joke, what do you think they would do to you for saying that?" Hopwell frowned. "I knew coming here was a mistake again. We should seal this room up and never come back. Forget it even exists."

"But…." Layten looked at the journal. He had to know. Hopwell didn't get it, he wasn't really going to be a Scholar. He and Wix though, they had the need. The drive to just 'know.' Not for power or money, but just the joy of learning. And to discover the truth. And the truth was there, right there.

"I can't. I have to know, Hop. You understand, don't you, Wix?" Layten asked his other friend, who was watching the blue corded journal with a hawk-like gaze.

"Oh? Yes. Yes." Wix smiled.

"And what if none of this is true?" Hop tried again.

"You'd be learning lies."

Layten knew that was a weak argument. And Hop knew it too. "Look around you. If these were lies, why place them here. Why put them behind a door with its own ward, that black orb? And why put its own guardian here for just this room. The only other guardian in this place makes sense, this one though?"

"What other guardian?" Hopwell turned to Layten. "Is there something you've not told us?"

"Oh." Layten felt foolish. "Early on. Before you arrived. Eimin the Annoying sent me through the temple here. There's a guardian there. It normally hides when we are in there, in the ceiling." Layten shrugged. "Sorry I didn't mention it before."

"What are you talking about? There's no guardian in the ceiling in the temple." Hopwell had dropped the anger in his voice. "What?"

"Layten, you are very confusing. The ceiling in the temple is normal." Wix tapped his chin. "Are you joking with us?"

Layten didn't know what to say. He never brought up the ceiling, he just assumed it was a feature of the temple. Try to rouse some piety by showing power. The idea that they didn't see the place the same way as him was worrying. "It's hard to explain," he finally said. "For me, when I enter the temple here, there's no ceiling. It stretches out into the darkness. Somewhere, up there the guardian lives. It's a half spider, half snake-looking thing. It spoke to me and sent me away. Said I wasn't in the right place, which I wasn't, thanks to Eimin." Layten frowned. "You know, for all the headache he gave me the first few days, he's also kind of vanished."

"That's because he works mostly with the Journeymen," Hopwell answered. "But stop trying to change the subject. You're saying that for you the temple looks different than it does for us?"

"I guess?" Layten shrugged. "It's like that orb. I hate it. It makes me feel cold, empty. Almost hungry. Just like that Anchor's staff."

"What staff?" Hopwell shook his head. "Do you have more you haven't told us?"

Fool. In a short span of moments, you've let them both know about things you were going to keep quiet.

Layten smiled. "Is it important?"

"It can't hurt to know." Hopwell sat down on the cold stone floor. "All of it."

Wix joined him, his characteristic grin gone. "Yes. Share."

Layten almost groaned. This wasn't important. That book was important. But without Hopwell and Wix on his side, he'd be in a worse place than he was now.

"Fine. Short version.

"I came here with an Anchor, and his two Protectors. We spent a night in a harbor, in Giller. That's where the book of Protector forms came from. And that white journal I have? I also grabbed a scroll, but I keep forgetting to look at that. Fine? Happy?" Layten wanted to remember as little as possible about the trip here. There were gaps. The fact that there were gaps made him fairly sure that parts of his memory had been erased or taken from him. And he didn't like the idea of that, at all.

"Anchors do not take people with them," Hopwell scowled. "Why was an Anchor anywhere near you?"

"My parents' workshop. It has a dispensation. It has its own warding circle. But those have to be replaced. Anchor Fean was there to replace it." Layten scuffed the floor. "He knew my parents. How I don't know. In the end, for some reason we had to hurry, and we used some kind of gateway. I don't remember much of that; they gave me something to drink beforehand."

Wix shook his head. "Layten, my friend. You need to tell stories better. But it is a quite strange story."

"It's impossible, that's what it is." Hopwell stood, brushing dust off his robes. "What did you say his name was, this Anchor?"

"Fean. He never gave a last name." Layten didn't get what Hop was getting at. "Why does it matter?"

"And the protectors, one man, one woman?" Hop asked again.

"Yes, Wilk and Binin." Layten was tingling. The hair on his arms and neck was standing straight up.

"That's the Navigator. The LEADER of the Anchors. The leader of all the Anchors brought you, a merchant's son from Lowter all the way here? And used a gate of some kind?" Hop was staring at Layten.

"He's what?" Layten didn't know how to respond to that. "He probably just told me that name as a joke. And there have to be other Anchors who have a man and a woman as Protectors."

"Right… what did he look like?" Hopwell pushed. "I've seen the Navigator once."

"I don't know," Layten shrugged. "He always had a hood on. Always."

"You do not think that was strange?" Wix chimed in. "I do not know much about the Anchors, not nearly as much as Hopwell here, but this does sound odd."

"Well, yes, but…" Layten sighed. "Look, I don't know much more than that. They were all nice enough."

"What did they have you drink?" Wix asked. "You said they had you drink something."

"Some vial. Purplish liquid? Tasted horrible. They said it was so the gateway wouldn't bother me. I don't know what that meant either." Layten sighed. "I know I am not giving you all many details, but I don't KNOW many details. There are gaps anyway."

"Gaps?" Hopwell stood brushing his legs off. "What do you mean gaps?"

"Gaps. Like things had been erased, or I'd been made to forget." Layten shook his head. "Turns out my parents had my memory erased when they would install the warding circle every year. So it didn't upset me, or something."

Hopwell gave him a long look that Layten could not place. Horror? Anger? Sorrow? He didn't know how to read that face. Wix was frowning, but that was it.

"What?" Layten finally asked.

"Layten… erasing memories is something that Anchors only due in very dire circumstances. There are only three or four Anchors who can do it. One being the Navigator. The others are high-ranking officers. And you said they did this yearly??" Hopwell scowled.

"Yes. I didn't know that until I was leaving, mind you. I was very angry at my parents for that, at least at the time." Layten didn't like learning any of this. He'd thought he'd put all that Anchor nonsense behind him. He was a Scholar or would be anyway.

"None of this makes sense." Hopwell helped Wix up after he'd offered a hand to the still seated man. "No sense at all."

"Maybe I'll find some answers in Jinir's journal. He founded the order after all, right?" Layten wanted to end all this speculation and focus on why they were here in the first place.

"What?" Hopwell shook his head. "Oh. I still think we should leave this room, seal that crack, and forget this place ever existed."

"You, my noble friend, are not a Scholar. You are a good man. You have a good heart. And a good mind. But you are not a Scholar. You do not have the thirst to understand. The thirst to *know*." Wix smiled at Hopwell. "It is not in your heart. With Layten and I it is different. It is part of our person. Part of who we are. We could not do what you suggest, no more than we could forget to breathe."

"Well said," Layten added, grateful that Wix was able to put it into words far better than he could.

"Right." Hopwell sighed. "How about this then. I don't want to read anything, but I also don't want anyone to find YOU all reading anything. So, I'll go out into the hallway, the wooden one, and keep watch."

"Who could find this place?" Layten almost laughed.

"Wix did," Hopwell shrugged. "And remember, we have our strange and untruthful Trinil wandering around, somewhere. If he happens to show up, I'd like to talk to him."

"That, my friend, is a good idea." Wix waved Hopwell towards the crack. "Go, keep watch."

Layten waited as Hop squeezed his way out of the room and walked off, his footsteps barely able to be heard as he moved away from them. He approached the journal, excited and scared at the same time.

"Layten, wait." Wix spoke, his voice low. "I think Hop worries too much. But I also think he is sometimes right. This Anchor, Fean? Yes? Fean. That is dangerous. Playing jump stones with your memories and removing the parts they don't want you to have? Dangerous."

"Maybe. But that's in the past. I'm here now. I'm sorry I wasn't more forthcoming about how I got here, I just… people don't always judge Anchors kindly. I didn't want that to influence how you and Hop felt about me." Layten paused. "In many ways you all are the only friends I've ever had. I grew up on the marsh, Wix. The village kids didn't like me all that much, I was different. I didn't live in town."

"Ha!" Wix grinned. "Truth, you and Hop are the first people I've trusted in a long time. Growing up on the streets of Ture is not a nice place. Even less nice if you have a strange name, with a strange accent. Often, I was chased by bigger people screaming that I was a spy from the south, or worse."

"Sorry. I didn't know that." Layten WAS sorry. "That must have been hard."

"Yes, and no. I learned to escape. I learned to run. I learned to hide. I learned other skills, like the opening of locks." Wix brushed his hands on his robe before putting a hand out. "Know this, Layten Grayread, you are my friend now, and always in the future. I trust you with my life."

Layten looked at the hand. He'd just wanted to come here to read a book. Granted, a book that was potentially going to undermine everything he'd ever been told or learned about his faith, and the fall of the City. How had it come to Wix doing THAT? With a start he realized that his friend was waiting for him to shake his hand. He did so, giving it a firm shake.

"Good. I was worried for a moment, Layten, I thought I was going to have to make other plans, you knew too much." Wix grinned.

Layten smiled back. "Well, I'm glad it didn't come to that. But can I read now?"

"Oh yes, I will read as well." Wix waved him towards the journal.

Layten approached the blue corded volume and slowly undid the knot he'd done last time, the cord velvety smooth under his fingers. The cord fell away without a sound, leaving the book closed, its nearly cold surface beckoning Layten to discover the truth, the real truth. He knew Hop was wrong about the room being set up to remove lies. That didn't make sense. No, these books were being protected. Someone had put this room together. A great many years ago. Someone had built this and hidden it away. To preserve the truth. They had hidden it to keep it safe, so that maybe, someday, someone would find it, and know.

Layten smiled. He was that someone. Wix was that someone. In a way Hopwell was that someone. He opened the book and began to read.

Chapter Twenty-Nine

Today, I tracked them down. Myriam VolFar and William Reis. They were living in the Reach, or what was left of it. I think they were both shocked to see me. I understand their reaction. I was a link to the City. To the past. To the before time. I didn't tell them what I did now. They probably already knew, the words of the 'High Prophet' of Sartum have already been spread from one end of the North to the other.

Why did I track them down? It wasn't to turn them over to Sartum. I joined Sartum because I was scared. Because I'm a coward. Not out of love, or belief, but just plain fear. I play my part, and I am rewarded for it. I think Sartum knows that I don't believe, or even like him, or her, or whatever it is. I make a useful mouthpiece, and he allows me to live and, even in some ways, prosper.

Myriam nearly charged at me with her hammer. She still had the changes from her self-healing. Brown hair and a strong body from smithwork, transformed into silverly white hair and a thin almost wraith-like appearance. Her eyes, once brown, now nearly a white blue. But it was her. William still looked the same as the few times I had seen him. Strong, steady. He was starting to gray though, his hair thinner.

They both had demanded to know, why am I here? After Sartum had smitten the Reach and named it forbidden, almost everyone had left who was still alive. I do not know if Sartum even checked to see if they were living there. For a god, Sartum is not overly concerned with details.

I told them, of course. I came to apologize. To atone. I was so focused on my desire to rejoin the ranks of the Tarns, to punish Mikol, to reclaim what I thought was my position by rights… that I didn't see the danger. I did not see what I could have done differently, and still don't, that would have affected the outcome. But I still feel responsible. I will always feel responsible.

I don't think William believed me. He hefted a hammer a few times; a hammer on which I could see the telltale signs of magic. Not strongly, but it was there. Myriam, however, finally lowered her guard enough to tell me 'thank you.' It's not much, but it helps. Myriam had the glow about her as well. Weaker by far than in the City, but still they had managed to figure out how to use the power that they had unleashed into Alos.

I left them there then. The pair of them, living in the ruins of the Reach. I have wondered if they stayed there, or did they leave finally, wandering out into the world. These lands hate them, and the south doesn't trust them. What must it be like to know, anywhere you go, someone wants you gone? It's the only reason I stay in the North. Because after all this time, I'm still a coward. I'm still scared.

Layten pushed the book away, trying to absorb this. The High Prophet Jinir had found the betrayers? And let them go? And of all places, the Reach? Every northerner knows that the Reach and the lands around it are forbidden to all. Stories abound about the horrible deaths that happen when you get too close to the ruins. Some say the ancient remnants of the Valni stalk the area, hunting any living thing that enters. Others say it's a curse, a curse that turns you mad, and makes you hurl yourself into the scar, or what had been the Mistlands, long ago.

Either way, it was a dangerous and evil place. A place that Sartum had rightly sealed away, a place he had made all the faithful avoid. And yet, the High Prophet had gone there. And had not died. Of course, he was the High Prophet. The founder of the Anchor order, even if he hadn't been one himself.

But the rest, that he didn't like Sartum? It made Layten's head hurt. Jinir was a revered figure, he who had turned his back on the evil and terror that was raw magic and became the light of the Unsundered God. He had loved Sartum, it was said. And one day he had marched off, alone, to spread the joy and light of Sartum to all the corners of Alos, never to be seen again.

Journey day, the day he'd left, was even celebrated in some parts of the North as a holiday, that same Jinir had hated it? None of it made sense. At all. Layten closed the journal and wondered if Hop was right maybe. These books were dangerous. Maybe this knowledge was too much for people. Maybe it would be better to seal this place up and forget it.

"Layten?" Wix asked from a different table. "Do you hear that?"

Layten tried to focus on what Wix was saying, and then realized that he did hear something. A series of thumps and maybe something else? He realized that Hopwell was out there. And something had to be wrong. "Hop!" Wix, to his credit, jumped into action. The smaller man was quicker and was already through the crack and out into the stone hallway before Layten could even get a few steps. The closer Layten got, the more he could hear it. Fighting. Someone, or some ones, was fighting!

Layten squeezed through the crack, hearing more than a few people cursing and running. In his rush he managed to rip his robe again, but that was the least of his worries. Bursting through the rest of the crack he was greeted by the sight of four people fighting Hop and Wix.

People was an unusual word. They weren't human. None of them were. One was a strange figure, its skin was jet black, and it appeared to have no face! One was huge, easily the largest living thing that Layten had ever seen personally, and the last two were Trinil. And even more surprising, one was the mysterious Trinil, Master Retuin.

Hopwell was thrusting and dancing back, hitting the other Trinil with a long stick, which looked surprisingly like a chair leg. It probably was a chair leg, none of them had weapons on them, or at least he thought so. Hop had managed to contact the knee, and that Trinil went down hard, cursing in some strange tongue and grabbing at the place it had made contact.

Wix was keeping both the faceless thing and the huge figure occupied. He was holding something sharp in each hand, that to Layten appeared to be marking rods. Wix dodged back from a mighty swing from the large creature, nearly tripping over his robe.

"LAYTEN, HELP HERE!" Wix yelled as he stumbled backwards.

"Help him!" Hop yelled keeping himself between the opening to the stone hallway and the two Trinil. "I can keep them busy!"

Layten ran towards Wix, intent on helping him. He however was so focused on the fight he ran close to the warding orb, far closer than he'd ever been. The feeling of icy cold engulfed him, and he nearly threw up with the surge of hunger that came with it.

I can help them. Let me help you. We can help you. We hunger. We starve. The voice came again, louder, stronger than before. *You can help us feed... after so long... feed.* A gnawing grasping desire filled Layten. His vision was gone. He could hear the fight but couldn't see anything but blackness. A deep never-ending dark. And cold... so cold...

A yell came from outside the dark, a yell that had to be from one of his friends. He knew it. Fear bloomed, driving away the gnawing pain that had filled his gut. *We can help, let us help...* Layten blinked, and the darkness faded. He was still moving, somehow, and was now heading straight towards the faceless thing. For a moment he wished he had a chair leg like Hop, or even marking rods like Wix did. He had neither, so he did the best thing he could think of. Arms outstretched, he launched himself at the strange figure, hitting it where it wasn't facing, hoping that it was a blind side. Two things became obvious. One, it very much had been the faceless form's blind side. Layten's tackle brought the creature down, and they both slammed into the wall. The faceless thing let forth a high-pitched whine that would have been painful, if Layten wasn't already in pain. Because the other thing that was obvious was that this thing, whatever it was, was solid. The impact of hitting it still reverberated through Layten's shoulder. He didn't THINK anything was broken, but he was going to have one massive bruise, assuming he lived through this.

He barely had time to think when the creature tried to slam a fist into his side. Thankfully the angle was all wrong, and the blow just barely clipped him. That glancing blow brought a searing pain with it as some skin was damaged strictly by the friction of the slight hit. Layten struggled to get a good grip on the thing, unsure of what to do next.

If he let go, the thing would attack him. But then he could help the others. He also wasn't sure just how long he could hold the creature. It was strong, and was starting to thrash about, making it even harder for Layten to keep his grip. He attempted to clear his mind, remembering a passage about focus in that Protector book they had been practicing from.

He concentrated on his breathing, making sure he didn't hold his breath and weaken his body because of it. One glance over showed that his friends were still moving. Wix had managed to score some hits on the large one; there was dark brownish red blood dripping from a few places on its arms. Hop was involved in using his makeshift weapon to block a series of attacks by the Ink Master, who, unlike all the others, was armed with an actual weapon. The silvery sheen of a sword was almost a blur in the Trinil's hands as it thrust and sliced at Hopwell.

Hop was more than holding his own, though from the gritted teeth and sweat that Layten could even see from here, he wasn't having an easy time of it. A searing line of fire brought Layten back to his own struggle as the faceless form dug its fingers into his wrist. Each digit burned as it dug in, and Layten half wondered if the thing was going to just rip his hand off.

Layten tried to roll, to both dislodge the grip of the thing, and to get better leverage. But the creature was ready for that, and somehow managed to push Layten upwards in the roll, making him flip over onto his own back and losing his grip.

Layten hissed as added pain came, this time from slamming his back onto the hard floor. He braced as the faceless creature raised a fist to slam it into his face, rather wishing for just a moment that he'd stayed away from this place.

The blow came, and the edges of his vision blurred with the hit. Another hit came into his gut this time, bringing a wave of nausea and a gasping escape of breath that he struggled to refill. "HOLD." The yell came as the creature raised another just black fist over him.

Layten tried to take a deep breath, but that brought a round of coughing that just made him feel worse. Still, he managed to blink away enough moisture from his wet eyes to see who had spoken. It was Master Retuin. He'd managed to disarm Hop, and had the young noble down on his knees, the point of the sword the Trinil held resting in the hollow of his throat.

Wix had stopped and the giant angry figure scowled at the smaller man, blood flowing more freely from three or four obvious stab wounds. The other Trinil, the one that Hop had managed to take down, was up, but limping. That Trinil spat at Hopwell, glaring at his friend with open hate.

"Good. Now, no one must die here today. No one at all. No one even has to be hurt more. I must thank you, young Grayread. You led me right to the one place I've been trying to find." Master Retuin smiled. "I didn't think it would be so soon however."

"What?" Layten finally managed to get enough breath to talk. "How?"

"No. I'm not going to tell you anything." Master Retuin gave that overly practiced smile again. "Now, your new friend there will enter the vault of secrets and retrieve a single book for me, and then we will be on our way."

Chapter Thirty

The strange creature rose up and gave Layten a swift kick as soon as it did so, drawing a new fresh wave of pain and more coughing. Layten hated the thing already. He had no idea what it was, but it was strong, and it had bested him. Layten had not expected to be in a fight at all, even less so in a fight with this strange being.

"Don't hurt our friend there. He's the only reason we found this place now." Master Retuin sighed. "And I thank you for that. I had hoped you might help us cut some possibilities, but you had already found it."

"Why are you looking for this place?" Wix asked keeping his eyes on the large form in front of him. "What are you after?"

"Same reason you all came back here. Knowledge. This is just very old, very secret knowledge." Retuin shrugged. "I had need of it. We had need of it."

"Who is we?" Hop asked, staying very still as the point of the sword was making a very small indent on his throat.

"Another thing I'm not going to tell you." Retuin nodded to the stone hallway that was still open. "Go on, you know what we are looking for."

The faceless figure half ran into the hallway and vanished into the dim light.

"You have made a mistake. You cannot take the books from that room." Wix edged away from the hall, and the door with the orb.

"You mean the guardian? Yes, I know it exists. Do you know how old that guardian is? It is one of the first ones made by your god after the fall of the City. He stole the idea and made it his own. Is that a little piece of knowledge they hide from you?" Retuin smiled. "I planned for the guardian."

Retuin looked down at Hopwell. "I did not plan on the three of you being as stubborn as you are. But here we are, and I have been successful in my task."

"We should just kill them," the other Trinil finally spoke. "Makes everything simpler."

"I would agree with you, but our partners do not want them dead. I believe they have some plans for one or all of them." Retuin shrugged. "But they may die anyway, after…."

Layten wanted to ask what he meant, but a sound came, a massive cracking as the door with the pillar shuddered. Moving fast enough that he wasn't fully seen, the faceless figure ran out of the stone hallway and paused only to nod at the Ink Master.

"Time for us to go." Master Retuin pulled a small sphere out of his pocket, throwing it at a nearby dim light that exploded into brilliance.

Layten covered his eyes in reflex, as the door behind him groaned and popped as a rivet or three gave way. The icy cold feeling came back, and the gnawing hunger, but no voices, not now. Blinking, Layten could see that the door was already half destroyed. And the guardian inside was slamming its huge metal fists into the back of the door.

"We have to run!" Layten managed to croak out pulling himself onto all fours. It hurt to breathe, it hurt to move, but dying to that thing would hurt even worse.

Hopwell and Wix were still blinking off the effects of that light but managed to get up and get to Layten as the next round of blows brought the door nearly fully off its torn hinges. "Come on!" Hopwell yelled as he and Wix helped Layten up and they broke into a run.

Layten gasped as he ran, still trying to regain some breath after the beating he'd gotten from the faceless thing. A huge boom echoed behind them, bringing extra speed to their steps. A crunching sound came from behind them, the sound of stone breaking.

"Run!" Wix yelled as all three made a mad rush to get out of the way of the guardian.

"Is it even after us?" Layten managed to yell. He was getting faster in the run, though one arm was glued to his side, holding an injury.

"Do you want to ask and find out?" Wix yelled back. "I do not, Layten. I do not at all."

They slammed through another hallway, hearing tearing and smashing sounds as the metal guardian tore the halls apart as it moved forward. Layten did not dare to look backward. He had no desire to see just how close the thing might be.

"Where are we going??" Layten yelled. "We can't just run forever!"

"Follow me," Hop screamed as he switched the direction he was running, heading towards...

Layten gasped as he figured out where Hopwell was going. Would that even work? It was smart though. The three of them stood no chance against this thing, even if it wasn't after them. He just hoped he'd live through this day, and maybe, just maybe get some answers after all this was over with.

"Ah!" Wix grinned as he ran. "A very good idea, Hopwell. A grand idea."

"I hope!" Hop yelled as he opened a door and ran into the one place that might offer a solution, the temple of Sartum.

Navigator Fean, leader of the Anchors, was angry. The speed in which this Priest, this 'Voice of Sartum' had taken over nearly everything he'd tried to build had been frightening. He'd had finally gotten an organized method for finding the southern intrusions into the northland, and now, all of that information flowed to that fool of a Priest, and before it got to himself. That was the truly dangerous part. The 'Voice of Sartum' getting access was bad enough; he'd already had to deal with half a dozen pointed letters and complaints about how the Anchors weren't doing their jobs, how slow they were to react to threats, and the like. What this Priest and those like him did not understand was just how being an Anchor affected you. They didn't understand the creeping madness that came with every use of your gift. They didn't understand the cost to stay focused on the here and now. They didn't see how the burden each Anchor carried inside them grew and grew with every encounter. They just saw someone with the staff and their Protectors making the evil power go away. And then they hated that person for having to deal with it.

But now, with this new player getting access to the information first, he was having to find ways to get Anchors to places faster. The portals were useful, but they extracted a toll. First, it accelerated the madness within, and second, it extracted a cost on their minds and souls. The darkness the portals traversed held things. Things that knew you. Things that knew your very soul. Things that hated you and would speak to you.

Fean hated the things. He'd used two getting Layten to the House of Knowledge, and that had almost been far too many. The night he'd gotten back here he'd shivered half the night, remembering the things the voices had said. His betrayals. His faults. His fears. Even the ones he'd forgotten. Every scrap of everything he'd ever done wrong. And how it made the other people feel, not in words, but the actual feelings.
This 'Voice,' though, appeared to have purposefully delayed getting information to him a few times already. Sightings of a blue fire in a forest? He didn't find out for three days afterwards. By the time an Anchor got there, a whole nest of Beelik had been established. That Anchor had hit their limit, and after the cleansing of the area, had been forced down into the descent, with her Protectors. If he'd known about it sooner, it wouldn't have been so much. That Anchor might still be here.
The worst was the reports of people using magic. The Anchors took those very seriously. If found to be true, the Anchor would capture them, and use the staff and a rite given to them from Sartum on high to burn the ability out of them.
But now? Not a single report had reached him of someone using magic. Not a one. He normally got at least rumors fairly often. Usually, it was nothing. A report made in anger, or in jest. But now? Not a single one. Which meant, this Voice person was intercepting them. Why?
Fean didn't have answers. And he hated that he didn't have them. The anger brought forth a giggle and he, without realizing it, jabbed a marking rod into his finger, the bright red spot of blood bringing a single glimpse of clarity.

He was close. So close. Soon he'd have to take the descent. But not yet. He had to hold on. He had to stop the drumbeat of war. He just had no idea how.

Chapter Thirty-One

Layten followed Hopwell and Wix into the temple, acutely aware of the sound of tearing wood and crunching stone that was moving up on them. The temple was empty, as it usually was. The House of Knowledge might be one of the five, but in many ways, it was the least… pious of the Houses. There had been a few things that had taken place here, but there wasn't a Priest assigned here, at least right now.

"I hope your guardian here can help!" Hop yelled as the door they had entered through flew apart as the one chasing them smashed it into pieces.

Wix yelled something that Layten wasn't even sure was a language and went down, a large shard of wood slashing through his cheek. Red blood welled up and began spilling onto the floor. Layten ran over, tearing the sleeve off his robe to use as a bandage.

Wix was rolling on the floor, grabbing at the wound. The movement was just making a greater mess as blood got more places. Layten tried to haul him up and held the torn robe to Wix's face. "Hold that there!" Layten had to yell as the stone wall around the now destroyed door shuddered and released puffs of stone dust.

Layten could hear other people now. The noise had attracted a large number of them. He couldn't see anyone though. He heard someone yelling for people to move back, to leave, too... Layten couldn't hear anymore as the wall shuddered again and part of it collapsed.

"Where is it??" Hopwell yelled looking up. "Should we try to make a run for it?"

Layten looked up as well, helping Wix cover the wound
on his face. The darkness stretched out to his vision.
Empty and black, he wanted to jump into it for some
reason. Jump into it and float away. The next blow
made the whole room shake and brought him back to
the now.

"No! if we run it will just keep chasing us. I don't know
why it's chasing us anyway. We didn't take a book!"
Layten knew that there wasn't any place they could run
to that would be safe anyway. Even leaving the House
of Knowledge wouldn't be safe. He had no doubt that
this thing, this strange ancient guardian would follow,
and they would fall exhausted long before it would.

"I'm not ready to die here, Layten!" Hop yelled.

"How's Wix?"

"Alive," Wix croaked. "My good looks are ruined
now!"

Layten almost laughed. Of course, they were all about
to die and that took most of the humor away, but still,
trust Wix to make him smile at a time like this. The
room shuddered again, and the book guardian rolled
into the room. Its coppery metal body covered with dust
and debris, but still looking fully whole. It raised its two
large arms, almost seeming to draw them back like a
bowstring, prepared to smash them into the stone floor.
Layten closed his eyes. He was about to die. He didn't
want to see it happen. He heard a whirring sound and
felt a massive rush of wind and then… a huge crash of
metal. "I guess you were right!" Hopwell yelled, which
made Layten open his eyes to a wonderful sight.

The temple guardian had arrived. It appeared to have slammed its tail into the book guardian, nearly breaking one of the large heavy arms off when it did so. That arm hung limp, torn metal and strange lights marked the spot where the damage had happened. Layten fleetingly wished he hadn't closed his eyes, he should have watched that happen.

The book guardian had rocked back with the blow and was unsteady, a fact that the temple guardian took advantage of. The tail flowed through the air fast enough for the rush to be heard and felt. Point first, it tried to smash the orb in the middle of the other guardian, but its opponent was ready for it, just the same. One of the smaller arms managed to grab the tip, wrenching it upwards and into the side of the thing. It plowed into the older guardian, tearing a new hole. The temple guardian attempted to pull the tail back for another attack but couldn't. The tip was stuck.

That was the only opening the book guardian needed. The surviving giant arm smashed down, claw-like, tearing at the tail mid-point. It ripped a large metal plate off the thing, along with a collection of wire, gears, and some yellow glowing fluid. The arm struck again with a sound of tearing and broken metal. This time doing more damage as it struck the same point. It ripped off even more strange parts, leaving everything past that point suddenly unable to move.

"We should get out of here!" Hopwell bellowed. "They are tearing each other apart, but I don't want to end up dead from getting hit in the head by some guardian's bad throw."

"Take Wix!" Layten pushed the smaller man towards Hop. "Get him some help."

"What about you?" Hop pulled Wix and helped the smaller man hold the now blood-soaked robe arm to his face. "I'm not leaving you here to die!"

"I'll be fine," Layten yelled. And he would be. He had no idea how he knew, but he knew he'd be all right. "Go! Wix has lost a lot of blood." That was true, the smaller man was stained red from his face down his whole side, it was a gruesome sight to see on his friend. Hopwell grimaced. "Fine. But don't die, Layten, I don't want to have to find a new Scholar!" He pulled Wix away, towards the other door, and away from the two large metal beasts fighting.

And the fight did continue. The temple guardian gave a large heave with what remained of its tail, and the rest of it tore off, spraying things that Layten hoped weren't poisonous or painful around the area. A spring, yellow and black, struck Layten on the hand, the pointed end of wire on one end embedding itself in his skin. Wincing, Layten yanked it out, thankful it wasn't anything like what had happened to Wix.

The ancient guardian moved forward, ignoring Layten, who sent a silent prayer of thanks to Sartum for that small miracle. The book guardian sent a series of hammering blows at the temple guardian. Each blow reverberated around the room, the sound of dented metal and broken machinery coming with each blow. The temple guardian jumped back on its strange spider-like legs, trying to coil what was left of the tail behind it.

Dodging an attack, the temple guardian swung the tail stump like a club. While it wasn't nearly as long as it had been, it was still strong. It hit one of the smaller arms, and completely broke it off. The arm flew across the room, breaking a few chairs and benches.

Layten suddenly doubted his earlier certainty that he wouldn't be hurt. One flying arm like that one hitting him would mean no more Layten. Or rather several much smaller parts of Layten. He ran then, not out of the room, but behind a large stone pillar that took up space by the door the older guardian had torn down. He could have made a run for it out that way, there was no door to stand in his way, nothing to stop him. But he wanted to stay. He had to know who won. How to document this battle. No living Scholar had ever seen two guardians fighting like this. He doubted anyone had in generations, if ever.

No, it was his job as a member of the House of Knowledge to study this. To know this. Even if he wanted to run away and pee himself in terror. He was scared. Part of him was at least. A more rational part of him was in control right now, but he knew if he lived through this he was going to collapse in exhaustion.

The temple guardian struck again, knocking the older model back again. While it was balanced on a massive orb, it did seem unsteady on it. Like any sufficiently large hit would make it move backward on the ball. But this time the older unit was somewhat better prepared, catching the tail stump with its lone working large arm and hand.

The two units seemed to struggle, sparks, strange fluids, and a loud whirring sound came from both the combatants. The sound only grew louder as they strained against each other, neither fully able to disarm the other. Soon the whirring sound was almost louder than the sounds of the fight itself, as fewer and fewer metal plates fell.

Then slowly, almost imperceptibly, the temple guardian was forced backwards and lower. The book guardian almost seemed to hunch over its opponent now, as it pushed the tail stump down and backwards, the occasional popping sound coming from the joints of the larger arm.

Layten was shocked. He was still going to die. This book guardian would defeat the temple one, and then come for him. He braced himself for the end of the newer guardian. A massive crack echoed through the room, and the whirring sound, just moments before so loud as to almost make it unable to hear, was gone. Layten blinked, unable to make sense of what he was seeing. The older unit was slumped over, just like he had been in the room with the books. Except… there was a single change. The green orb in its middle was not green, or even faintly glowing. It was dark, cold. How had that happened?

His question was answered as a long sharp-tipped spider-like leg pulled itself out of the book guardian. Layten knew then what had happened. The temple guardian had gotten the ancient model to overcommit, and it had used that mistake to break the orb with one of its legs.

Layten was safe. Hop was safe. And Wix would survive, he was sure of it. The energy he'd been feeling left him then, and he slumped to the floor.

"You should not be here." The temple guardian spoke, its 'face' turned toward Layten. "This is not your place."

"I know... I know..." Layten managed to gasp. Right after that, he wished he wasn't there. As into the now ruined temple strode the head of the House of Knowledge. Grand Scholar Dar. He was flanked by several other senior Scholars, and all were wearing some degree of anger and horror at what they were seeing.

"What exactly did you DO?" Grand Scholar Dar looked down at Layten, his face frowning and as dark as the storm clouds over the marsh back home.

Layten struggled to come up with an answer. He hadn't done anything really. He'd just run. He'd run because they were being chased. Hop had led them here, but it had been a good idea. One that had saved their lives, though Wix had been hurt.

"We ran here," Layten finally said. He knew that was a not very clear answer. But he didn't know enough right now to give one he thought would be accepted. Was there any way to come up with one that would be? The realization of what had happened settled over him. He was going to be kicked out, at the minimum. If Hop was right, and there were still the Chastisers around, he'd have a lot worse than having to travel home to his failure.

And he hadn't even done anything but save his own life! "We ran to save our lives," Layten added, watching the incredulous stares as the Scholars waited for a better answer. "I am sorry. But can we go someplace else to answer questions?" Layten felt horrible. He was covered with dust and dirt and sweat, he'd just missed being killed, and the only thing he could think of was having to explain to his parents how he'd been kicked out. They might even stop doing business with his father. That would ruin them.

And it would all be his fault.

Chapter Thirty-Two

"That's your best answer?" the Grand Scholar finally spoke. "You ran? That's it?"

"Please, can we go somewhere else, I'll tell you everything. The whole story." Layten wanted to be anywhere other than right here. His strength was leaving him, and he wanted to sit. He needed to sit.

"Fine. Come. You can join the other two and we WILL get to the bottom of this." Grand Scholar Dar led the way out of the ruined temple, followed by Layten, who discovered he was unable to walk without limping. His hip hurt. He didn't remember it being injured, but so much had happened. Who knew what the truth was with that?

Layten was led through a hallway; on the far end were several students being held back by unfamiliar men in unfamiliar armor. He could see their faces, some pale, some not. Some frowning, some smiling and whispering. And then he saw Delerie. To his eyes she seemed worried. Even distraught. It didn't matter though. He'd never see her again. He turned his head away, just wanting this all to be over.

They stopped at a door that was marked by a gold seal, which opened to a room with a large wooden table, and a dozen chairs. He was happy to see that Hopwell was here, and Wix! Wix had half his face bandaged, and both his friends were pale and exhausted to the eye, but they were alive.

"Ah, Layten! Good to see you." Hop tried to put some bravado in his voice. "How was the fight?"

"Silence." Grand Scholar Dar and those with him sat at one end of the table, facing Hopwell, Wix, and the empty seat for Layten. "Sit there." He ordered, gesturing to the seat.

Layten almost sighed in relief at sitting down. His hip hurt worse, and he'd been sure a few times he was going to fall over. This was a hard wooden chair, but right now, it was the most comfortable seat he'd ever had.

"Now. Explain. Everything. Now. Half the House of Knowledge is destroyed. I have a half-broken guardian in the temple that is part of the destruction. I have some other guardian that I've never seen that is fully broken also in the temple. And I have the three of you who led that thing there." Grand Scholar Dar crossed his arms and sat back, his gaze almost wanting to make Layten get up and run away. Almost.

"It is my fault. A bit." Wix spoke first. "I found a place with books. Secret books. That guardian was protecting the books. If you tried to take the books, the guardian would stop you, see? Today, some people came, followed us. Or found us, not sure. They took a book. We ran, the guardian followed, and we led it to the temple, hoping the guardian there would save us." Wix's voice was flat and didn't sound right, until Layten realized that was probably because of the injury to his face.

"Why did the guardian of these 'books' chase you if you didn't take a book?" Scholar Nimer asked before the Grand Scholar could talk, who frowned at the question.

"I... I don't know." Layten cut off Wix who was about to answer. "It shouldn't have."

"What books were these? How did you find this place? What were you doing?" Grand Scholar Dar shook his head. "These answers do not make sense."

"They were forbidden books." Hopwell sat back in his chair. "Old books. Wix found them kind of by accident. He was… well…" Hopwell paused and gave Wix a shrug, who nodded back at him. "He was looking for a quiet place to spend with a girl."

That at least got a reaction, a smattering of slight smiles broke out among the older Scholars. Even the Grand Scholar raised an eyebrow at that fact. "Oh?" He finally said before seeming to brush it aside. "After we are done here, you will take us to these books."

"Yes, Grand Scholar." Hopwell lowered his head as he spoke.

Layten almost envied how calm Hopwell appeared. "One was a journal. Written by High Prophet Jinir." Layten added. "Others were the true history of the destruction of the City, or at least claimed to be."

The reaction was swift then. A few whispers back and forth grew to a murmur as the Scholars discussed this piece of information. Two stood up and started running in the general direction where they had come from. "Stop!" The Grand Scholar stood. "Silence! We will find the truth of that soon. But I want more information. Who took anything? You said someone found you?"

Layten nodded. "It was the Ink Master. Master Retuin. He, another Trinil, some… giant man, and a figure with black skin, and no face."

More whispers came then, and the Grand Scholar seemed to take that information even more seriously. "Are you sure?" He sat down and leaned toward Layten. "Absolutely sure?"

"Yes." Layten shrugged. "Why?"

"Scholar Nimer, go get the copy of the Races of 235lso. The… fourth edition." The Grand Scholar looked at Layten. "Explain more."

Layten watched as Scholar Nimer left to go get some book. "There is not much to explain. I don't know how they found us. They found us and delayed us enough for the faceless figure to enter and leave with something. Then that guardian thing was after us and we ran."

"You had met the Ink Master before, I take it?" Grand Scholar Dar kept his eyes on Layten.

"Yes. Twice. Once the first day I had gotten here. I came early. He was at the meal. Then not again for months, until a few days ago. He gave me a letter to give to my father. Something about needing special paper. The weird thing was the letter was blank. Just oily and strange." Layten paused. "And today, of course."

Oddly enough the mention of the letter got the most reaction. A Scholar that Layten didn't know leaned forward and whispered something to the Grand Scholar. "Is this letter still in your room?" The Grand Scholar frowned even more.

"Yes." Layten didn't know why that was important.

"Good." The Grand Scholar nodded to the Scholar who had asked, who then got up and left, walking quickly out. "We will retrieve this letter." Dar frowned again.

Layten looked over at Hopwell, who was sitting still with a small smile on his face. How he could smile at all at a time like this he didn't know. Wix, pale and dirty, and covered with a noticeable amount of dried blood, shrugged at Layten in response to Layten's look. His confusion was broken by the arrival of Scholar Nimer, carrying a large black-bound volume, who placed it on the table with a thud. She unbuckled its strap and opened it searching through it carefully before stopping. "There." She showed the page to the Grand Scholar.

The Grand Scholar read for a moment before turning the book to face Layten. "Did the faceless thing look like this?"

The book had a rather ornate and old engraving on it. But the figure was the same. Jet black skin, no face. It was crouched as well, giving it a look like a coiled spring, ready to strike. "Yes." Layten paused. "It was strong too. Far stronger than I expected. I tackled the thing, but it nearly killed me."

"Are you sure?" the Grand Scholar paused. "Absolutely sure?"

"Yes." Layten didn't understand. "What is it?"

"It shouldn't even exist. And not anywhere in these lands especially." The Grand Scholar turned the book back towards himself. "This is a Leuh. A race that is dead. Or should be dead."

"A leuh?" Layten had never heard that word before.

"They were the creation of the Nightmoon God. A dark and sinister race. There were never many of them, at least according to the histories. They all died very long ago, even long before the unsundering. In the time before." The Grand Scholar paused. "They were assassins. Killers. Bringing all other races to their creator."

Layten had heard of the Nightmoon God. Who hadn't? The god of the unbeliever dead. If you didn't follow a god, or didn't believe, when you died the Nightmoon God took you. This wasn't a good thing; this was no act of mercy. The Nightmoon God would slowly eat your soul, and you'd feel it. Every moment, stretching into untold time. But since the unsundering, no human would have anything to do with that. They had Sartum now. He protected his chosen people. And even before the unsundering, humans didn't have much to do with the Nightmoon God.

The Grand Scholar flipped through the book and paused, turning it around again. "And this? Does this one look like the large one?"

Wix leaned forward, "Yes. Not exact. But similar. Very strong. Very big. Not very fast. Thankful for that."

Grand Scholar Dar almost smiled again but hid it well before turning the book back. "A hybrid. Again, an impossibility."

"Hybrid?" Hopwell chimed in, his air of unconcern vanishing. "That can't possibly be true."

"I should have expected a Golon from Buniler would know what a hybrid is." The Grand Scholar shrugged. "It fits the description, and none of you have lied yet."

"But there hasn't been a hybrid since the fall of the City." Hop scowled at the book. "there's no way that can be accurate."

"I'm confused," Layten added. "What exactly is a hybrid?"

"And how do you know we aren't lying?" Wix added.

"Ah. Well, I'll answer the second question first. I am the Grand Scholar. My badge of office…," Dar tapped a medallion he wore with a finger, "…allows me to know when I'm being lied to. A gift from Sartum." The Grand Scholar tapped the book. "As to the first question. As I'm sure your fellow troublemaker can inform you, back before the unsundering, in that evil den known as the city, hybrids were made. Mixes of races. An abomination to be sure. Only made possible by the power. They created the hybrids in horrible experiments. They were also supposed to be extinct."

Layten did not like the sound of that at all. Two supposedly extinct and dead races prowling around the House of Knowledge? "I don't… I don't know what to say."

"How did you know about the temple guardian?" The Grand Scholar addressed his question to Hopwell. "That feature is hidden from students. Until today I would have sworn that only I and the Gatekeepers knew of its existence."

"I…" Hopwell shrugged. "I didn't. But I trusted Layten, who knew it was there."

"Oh?" The Grand Scholar pushed the book off to the side. "You knew it was there. How?"

Layten felt a chill settle onto his bones. He hated talking about this. It reminded him of how Anchors made him feel... that gnawing emptiness. But the Grand Scholar had been fair so far, and he apparently would know if Layten lied anyway. "I spoke to it. I ended up there not knowing what it was, early on. It came down from that empty place and spoke to me."

The reaction from the Grand Scholar, and all the Scholars was not what he'd expected. If surprise had a face, that was what he was seeing now. The Grand Scholar grabbed the medallion he wore and squeezed it, his knuckles white. "What did it tell you?" He finally managed to ask.

"That I was in the wrong place. That I didn't belong there." Layten didn't understand why they were so surprised. "I agreed and I left."

The Grand Scholar shook his head and opened his mouth to speak when the Scholar who had left to get the letter returned, holding it in a gloved hand. "I was right, Grand Scholar." He placed the letter next to the book. "Oil of Gleengrass."

"What?" Layten was confused. "What is that?"

To his surprise, it was Wix who answered. "Ah. Nice trap." Wix shook his head and then raised a hand to his injured cheek. "Oil of Gleengrass. Trinil can smell it and track the path people have taken who have touched it. It has no smell to anyone who is not a Trinil. He soaked the paper with it and handed it to you. Even then he wanted to see where you went. You see?"

Layten looked down at his hand, rubbing his fingers together. "I see." He gritted his teeth. This Master Retuin had played him like a fool. There were still a great many questions, but some had been answered. They knew what the strange people with the Trinil had been, and how they had been tracked. It still didn't explain why the book guardian had followed them, or how the Ink Master had betrayed them all anyway. Hadn't they been told that the Priesthood had approved of the Trinil being here? And what book had they taken?

"Come." Grand Scholar Dar stood. "It's time to see this secret book location. I've got all the answers I can get from you."

Chapter Thirty -Three

"No, that won't be necessary," a new voice said as a small group of armed men entered the meeting room. Each was clad in the livery and colors of the Priesthood of Sartum.

Layten backed up, away from the door. Every instinct told him to run and run now. Every face of these newcomers was unfriendly, and in fact several of them looked rather…angry or maybe contemptuous, if that was the word.

"This is bad, Layten." Hopwell leaned over and whispered. "Why is the Church guard here? This isn't normal, and that worries me."

"I agree." Wix joined them, his voice low. "We see them in Ture. Sometimes. Very dangerous."

"I know, but I don't think we can do anything. Not now at least." Layten watched as a new player entered the room. Younger than Layten expected, but thin and pale. But not weak. Nothing about this man said weak. In fact, the opposite. This man commanded the room, and everyone knew it. He was dressed in dark red robes, with orange threads of some metal woven through them. But they were… disturbing to look at. Every step seemed to form shapes and images that were vaguely disturbing.

"Grand Scholar Dar." This Priest spoke slowly, his voice filling the room. "You have made grave mistakes, it seems."

"I am sorry, but who are you?" The Grand Scholar stood straight, his back stiff. "I am the Grand Scholar of the House of Knowledge. Founded by the Great Sartum. Here I am His voice; here I am His arm."

"No." The Priest smiled, but not a friendly one. "I am the Voice of Sartum. In ALL places." He reached under his robe and pulled out a dark metal rod. "Do you know what this is, Grand Scholar?"

Layten watched as Dar, who just moments before had been facing this newcomer down, shrank back. "It's a confessor rod. From before the unsundering."

"Exactly right. But I should expect that you, the Grand Scholar, would know of these I suppose. Wonderful tools, these confessor rods. I'm working on bringing them back you know? When people misbehave as horribly as you have, well… pain makes a wonderful curative. It brings them clarity, purpose of thought." The Priest held up the rod and whispered something. The rod reacted nearly instantly. The far end of the rod began to glow. Red, orange, yellow and then a nearly white color. Even from here Layten could feel the heat from it. And it scared him. It was obvious what it was for. He had no interest in being the one this strange and disturbing man wanted to use it on.

"This rod is over a thousand years old. We only have a handful left, at least for now." The Priest dropped his smile. "You have failed Sartum, Grand Scholar. As has the House of Knowledge. For a great many years our lord has watched and waited. But this… this betrayal, this evil you have harbored, this is too far for our Kind Lord to forgive." The Priest, without warning, jabbed the rod forward, the glowing end hitting the medallion that the Grand Scholar wore.

There was a noise not unlike a hot stone cracking, sharp and painful. The medallion cracked and fell apart, but the Priest wasn't done. He pushed the rod harder, the glowing end burning through cloth and into skin. The Grand Scholar screamed and writhed, but for some reason he could not move away. He was held fast, but in a great amount of pain.

Layten took a half step back again getting as close to the back wall as he could. This was horrible! The sound, and then the smell. Burnt roast it was, strong, and made him want to vomit. He choked it back, but Hop wasn't as strong stomached, and he retched hard, holding onto Layten's sleeve, the one he had left at least, for support.

"There." The Priest, this 'Voice of Sartum', removed the rod, and the Grand Scholar, or maybe former Grand Scholar, collapsed. "Do not worry, Dar. I am not going to kill you. In truth, no one here is going to die. At least, not today."

The Voice of Sartum faced the Scholars who regarded him with looks of horror and fear. "Know this! As of today, the Houses of the North are disbanded! Sartum has decided in his wisdom that the south meddled in the northlands too often, too much, too far. To this point, Sartum has launched a crusade. We shall march on the south. Not just a House, not just a city, not just a country, but the whole of the free lands. All the lands who have seen the power and the light of Sartum. We shall march on the south and put it to the torch. Every scrap of magic is to be destroyed. Every evil creature that depends upon that foul force is to be destroyed!"

The Voice spoke louder now. "We shall cleanse them. No more will we suffer these intrusions; no longer will we have to suffer the Anchors walking our roads and cities. They will lead the vanguard, and once the south is cleansed of the taint of magic. Once the south burns with our righteous purity. Once the people of the south have been properly chastised... the Anchor order will end. We will be free of their taint, once and for all."

"All races will follow Sartum or be put to the blood. Even as I speak, right this moment, the Church is taking every non-human in the North and questioning them. If they properly follow Sartum, new positions will be found to support the crusade. Those who do not..." the Voice paused.

"The House of Knowledge is no more!" The Voice proclaimed loudly. "In the morning, you will march out of this place. All of you. You will be joined by the City guard, and all able-bodied men and women. You will be trained, and then you will take part in the cleansing of the evil that for far too long we have allowed to fester. Say goodbye to this life, for Sartum has need, and you WILL answer!"

The Voice looked down at the still groveling Grand Scholar, who was curled up into a ball, still clutching in one hand the broken medallion of office. Layten could see the red forming around it as he grasped it so tight it cut into his hands, deeply. "Do not despair. You will still serve Sartum, and that should always be your goal." The Voice of Sartum nodded to his guards and they marched out, the steps echoing around the room, leaving a silence that no one wanted to fill, even if they could.

Layten, Hop, and Wix exchanged looks. Soldiers? Crusade? What was happening?

Navigator Fean read the report three times and almost threw up. He had failed. Just mere hours before, the so-called 'Voice of Sartum' had marched into the House of Knowledge and disbanded it. He had done the same at all the other Houses. How he was moving that fast was a question that Fean didn't want to know the answer to. The portals were supposed to be a gift from Sartum himself to the Anchors. If he'd granted that gift to this 'Voice,' that said a great many things that Fean didn't want to think about.

It was war. Not just war, but a crusade. A war to end the south. A war to end magic. This was a worthy goal of course. A great goal. But this wasn't the way. There was no way the North could wipe out all magic in the south. None. Even with every Anchor that still walked the lands, or even twice as many. Or even three times as many, there simply weren't enough people with the talent, with the right kind of mind.

No, something else was going on, regardless of what the Voice said. Fean knew it would only be a matter of time before the two of them would meet officially. He as the Navigator of the Anchors, and the 'Voice of Sartum' as the leader of the grand army of Sartum.

Even worse was the note attached that said Layten and some friends of his were involved in something that had happened before the Voice showed up. Two guardians fighting. A mess of destruction. One of Layten's friends had been injured, and the other… was a Golon?

Fean shook his head; he didn't have time to worry about that. He quickly wrote a series of notes to send out. He couldn't keep Layten safe in the House now. But he could do what was possible to keep him out of harm's way on the battlefield. He had to keep him off the front lines and away from any fighting. He had to.

"What are we going to do?" Wilk asked, perched on his windowsill as usual.

"Where's Binin?" Fean kept writing. "I don't want to have to repeat my orders."

"I'm here!" Binin broke in, already putting her armor on. "Is the rumor true?"

"Yes. It's war." Wilk frowned. "Or a crusade."

"It's stupid," Fean added, finally looking up. "Even if we had a thousand Anchors, there would be no way for us to remove that much magic. I do not understand the point of this. But this is what we are going to do…."

THE
END OF BOOK ONE
'SCHOLAR'

The story of Layten Grayread will continue in

THE ASCENDANT PATH: SOLDIER

About the author:

Josh Cook lives in sometimes sunny Florida with his wife and two children, one overly excitable dog and a cat who hates everyone. You can learn more at https://www.joshccook.com.

Other Books by Joshua C. Cook

The Forgemaster Cycle
Blood of a Fallen God
The Anvil of Souls
A City in Blue

The Bridgefinders Series
Bridgefinders
Bridgebreaker

Dust Ash and Sand
A Pact of Dust
An Agreement of Ash
The Price of Sand

Project: Perception
Canitus

You Wrote it! What to know before you self-publish.

GLOSSARY

Amder – The former god of craft and creation. Returned to existence by the efforts of the last Forgemaster, William Reis and his companions. Was later discovered that Amder and Valnijz were in fact what remained of the sundered god, name unknown. Split by the Vinik during the arrival of the 'gods' on Alos in an attempt to save their world.

Anchor – An order of those who banish or absorb 'free' magic. Founded by Sartum and High Prophet Jinir in the year after the destruction of the City in Blue. Anchors are both feared and celebrated by most northerners. They are hated in the south. Anchors can only deal with magic for so long before they go crazy and must enter something called 'the descent.'

Anchorhold – The headquarters of the Anchors, based on the old Smithing Guild of Palnor, in Ture.

Anvil of Souls – The birthplace of the gods. One place that magic runs powerful and free. It is now fully locked away by the gods, and mortals are unable to access it.

Buniler – A city on the east coast of the northern lands. A rich land, it is home to two things. The Dome of the Lords, where nobles from all the north meet when decisions that affect them, all are being made, and the Tower of Records, where all the records for the northlands are kept. There is a long-standing question as to why the records are there, and not in the House of Knowledge.

Chastisers – A secret order that existed at one time to root out heresy in the Church of Sartum. In the years during the wars of northern unification, the worship of Sartum was new. The Chastisers saw to it that all would follow the truth faith. There are persistent rumors that the order still exists in some form.

Confession rod – a tool of the Tempered, an order like the Chastisers but from the days of Amder in Ture. A footlong rod of metal that if you knew the right words could be made to have one end glow white hot to punish or destroy. Their creation was lost after the unsundering.

Construct – Large to giant machines powered by magic. They were invented in the City in Blue, and the secrets of their making was taken by Sartum in that conflict. No one is sure how many were made by the Unsundered god, but today they are rarely seen. It is rumored that every major temple and the Houses that were founded by Sartum have a construct somewhere on site.

Delerie Kilmeed – A red haired fiery young woman from Orbask, in the northern mountains. A student at the House of Knowledge as well.

Descent – a place in the Anchorhold where Anchors who have taken in too much power go with their Protectors. No one either knows or speaks about what happens there. But no Anchor or Protector who enters ever exists.

Fean – Fean is an Anchor who guided Layten on his way to the House of Knowledge. It is unclear what or how, but there is some connection between Fean and Layten's parents. He also is the Navigator of the Anchors, the leader of the order.

Flitter – strange magical creatures that seem to spring forth from nowhere fully intelligent and clothed. Only found in concentrations of magic, Flitters are blindingly fast, and avoid contact with humans most of the time. The few who had spoken to a Flitter say they are all annoyed by all mortals, not just humans.

Forsworn – a group of humans who all have the same look, and do not talk to anyone who is not a forsworn. They all have pale skin, and grey black hair. They almost always work as servants in the Houses or to the Priesthood. Questions about the origin of the forsworn are strictly forbidden.

Giller – a trading town on the border of Lowter and the far richer Vislin. At the crossroads of several trade routes.

Golon – a noble rank. Golon are rich, and pretty much can do what they want. They must answer to the Priesthood still. Most think of Golon as pompous and annoying.

Gorom – a race that is all but extinct in the north, the Gorom are a short squat pale race who traditionally lived deep underground and had a large dislike of everyone else. Sartum struck a bargain with their creator god, Grimnor to save them from extinction. The result was death of Grimnor, and the slow decline of the Gorom. It is unclear how many Gorom exist in the southlands.

Grobbin – a short green skinned and scaled primitive race of magical creatures. Grobbin are primitive but are known to swarm out of nowhere and capture and eat every single person they find. Grobbin are considered in the northlands to be a horror and are used to often scare children into compliance.

Harbor (Anchor) – the smaller meeting halls and waystations of the Anchor order. The Anchors have a strong nautical theme for reasons lost to time. In most cities and towns, the Harbors are off by themselves, and no one goes to near to it, resulting often in a large empty square or courtyard with the Harbor stuck right in the middle.

High Prophet Jinir – One a Tarn of the City in Blue, Jinir switched sides and became a follower of Sartum, renouncing his former ways. He was instrumental in the founding of most of the Houses and rites of the early Church of Sartum. He vanished one day and was never seen again.

Holant – a magical spirit that at first exists as a wispy thing, it raises a tree to inhabit when the time is right. Once it has joined with the tree, the tree is mobile and exhibits a startling amount of aggression as the Holant in spirit form are gentle and kind.

Hopwell Linew – A Golon from Buniler itself, Hopwell is handsome, and rather intelligent. He is currently on his rounding. Hopwell is a bit of a rouge but seems to have a good heart. He is often secretly very unsure of himself and his own decisions.

House of Blood – One of the Houses founded by Sartum and Jinir. The House of Blood is dedicated to fighting and warcraft. The strongest warriors and archers, the smartest tacticians are all from the House of Blood.

House of Craft – Another of the Houses founded by Sartum and Jinir. The House of Craft is where the finest craftsmen are trained. There are whispered rumors that the House of Craft wants the location of the Anchorhold due to its history. By size it is the largest of the Houses.

House of Healing – Another of the Houses founded by Sartum and Jinir. The House of Healing is dedicated to just that, Healing and medicine. Herbology, medicines, bone setters and the like. A few of the more advanced students are chosen to have the healing gift of Sartum and can use godly given magic to heal with.

House of Knowledge – Another of the Houses founded by Sartum and Jinir. The House of Knowledge is where secrets are kept, and all general knowledge, regardless of how esoteric it is, is kept. New research is done often, and required, often resulting in the oddest books and scrolls being made.

House of Song – Another of the Houses founded by Sartum and Jinir. The House of Song is centered around music. It is known, though not spoken about that most of the music that comes out of this House is based on propaganda about Sartum. Whispers say this is the only reason the House still exists.

Lowter – a very poor country on the far west coast of the northlands. Its coastline is almost entirely marshlands, and it possesses very little in the way of mineral wealth or any other valuable resource. It does contain a great deal of timber, but with better trees elsewhere, and the lack of infrastructure in Lowter, it is not harvested much. People from Lowter are often made fun of.

Myriam VolFar – One of the two betrayers at the fall of the City in Blue. She was the namer of Sartum but turned her back on the Unsundered god and with William Reis, released magic into the world, freely. She and William Reis vanished in the aftermath of that event.

Orbask – a mountain bound land locked country, Orbask is known for two things. The passions of its people, and it's intense dislike of magic in all forms. Even Anchors are spat on in Orbask, for going anywhere near magical power. Even god given magical gifts make them uncomfortable.

Palnor – Still the most powerful country in the northlands, Palnor is home to the Anchorhold and the Priesthood of Sartum. On the western side of the country lie the Skyreach mountains and the city of the Reach.

Pin needle – a strange tree with fine needle like leaves. They are short and start off rather bronze looking at their base before fading to a gray green. Pin needles were unknown in all Alos before the destruction of the City in Blue. For many years they were believed to be tied to magic and were burned down and destroyed. No link could ever be found, and eventually people stopped trying. Now considered just another tree.

Pol – a tiny dying village near the coast of Lowter. Once the sight of an army base during the northern unification war where all the lands of the north were brought under the thumb of the Church of Sartum. The only reason the village hasn't fully vanished is the Grayread workshop on the coast.

Protector – Every Anchor has two Protectors with them. Protectors are armed, and well-trained fighters. They exist to both keep Anchors safe from more mundane threats and to keep others safe from Anchors who have gone mad.

Reach – A city in the Skyreach mountains. It was ravaged in the rebirth of Amder, and then after the return of Sartum was shunned due to it being the home of William Reis. While a few stragglers still live there, it is considered a cursed place by many.

Retuin – a Trinil who works as the Inkmaster in the House of Knowledge. Claims to be a follower of Sartum.

Sartum – The Unsundered god. The remade god of Humans by Myriam VolFar in the Anvil of Souls. Sartum quickly took control of the human race and forged them into a powerful force for his will. There are rumors that the name Sartum was chosen by Myriam VolFar for a reason, but that reason has been lost to time. After unification wars, Sartum went mostly quiet, and has not been seen in physical form for hundreds of years.

The Rounding – an old tradition where a young Golon would, before joining the ranks of the decision makers would spend a year in each House. While once a common practice, the rounding has fallen by the wayside for most Golon. Only traditionalists keep to it.

Timik – a city on the Silverblood river, Timik is the location of the House of Knowledge. Timik grew around the House, and in most ways, the city revolves around it.

Trinil – a tall thin race, Trinil are the creations of the forest goddess. True Trinil can always know if someone is lying. Rarely if ever seen in the northlands like most non-human races, Trinil mostly live in the south.

Ture – The capitol of Palnor.

Valnijz – the Blood god, the god of rage and destruction. One half of Sartum. Destroyed in the events leading to the return of Sartum.

Vilom – a highly ambitious Priest who has been appointed as the 'Voice of Sartum' and now runs the Church, and through it the whole north of Alos.

Voice of Sartum – a newly created rank, above even the High Priest, the Voice of Sartum is the mortal representative of the gods will. At least according to the Voice.

Warding circle – A device created by the Anchors that drives magic away from a set area. Used by smaller villages and towns to keep the evil of magic at bay.

William Reis – the last Forgemaster of Amder, was part of the return of Sartum. Who along with Myriam VolFar betrayed the god Sartum and released magic into the world. Considered a great evil in the northlands. He vanished with Myriam VolFar. It is known that he is also hated in the southlands by most mortals, but NOT the intelligent magical creatures.

Wiximinon Quilit – a student at the House of Knowledge. He is from Ture but speaks with an unusual accent. His parents are from an unknown far-off land according to him, which accounts for the way he talks. He is a former gang leader and thief from the streets of Ture.